Jerry McAllister and the Slaves of the Tellusian Underground: Book One

Tad Parker, Jr.

Enjoy! Your Friend
Tad Parker, Jr

SD
SmallDogma Publishing

Small Dogma Publishing
Lakeland, Florida

Small Dogma Publishing

Lakeland, Florida 33804

Printed in the United States of America on acid free paper.

Cover Design by Small Dogma Publishing, Inc.

ISBN 978-1-935267-02-7

LCCN 2009925579

13 12 11 10 10 9 8 7 6 5 4 3 2

Congratulations! You are a LifeSaver!

Literally... by buying this book, you most likely saved a life. Small Dogma Publishing has committed to donate 50 cents from each book sale to the Feed the Children Campaign dedicated to end world hunger and poverty. Right now, a person dies every three seconds from starvation or poverty related illness... most likely a child under the age of 5. This child's death could have been prevented by pennies worth of food and medication.

What a tragedy it is that something so preventable is happening in such record numbers. And while 50 cents per book isn't much, it is something, and if we can all individually just do something, we can make a huge difference as a whole. If you would like to know more about ending hunger please visit www.feedthechildren.org or look for their link on www.smalldogma.com. Again, thank you for your support and enjoy your purchase.

Sincerely,

Matt Porricelli, M.B.A.
President
Small Dogma Publishing

To my wife, Cindy
Who had to put up with my insanity.
And to my sons
Who encouraged it.

Jerry McAllister and the Slaves of the Tellusian Underground: Book One

TABLE OF CONTENTS

PROLOGUE

Ten Years Ago
Christopher at the Well

"WHY DON'T YOU EVER LISTEN? I told you to tie that thing at least four or five times," Christopher barked. "You want me to drop to the bottom?"

Danny didn't answer. Instead, he moved in to tie the extra knots that secured the rope to the tree trunk.

Chris shoved him aside and continued his rant. "Jeesh. I thought you used to be a Scout."

Danny opened his mouth to say something, but thought better of it. When Chris got into one of these moods, it was better not to say anything.

Chris stomped over to the edge of the well, then snapped at one of the twins. "Darren, gimme that pack, will ya?"

Darren, the only redhead in the group, picked the old military bag that had belonged to Christopher's uncle and tossed it at him.

"Man! Be careful with that!" Chris said. "Sometimes I wonder how you guys had enough brains to survive this long. What if I hadn't caught it?"

He slung the dirty green pack over his shoulder and threw one leg over the edge of the well. With one leg dangling over the abyss, Chris thought, *I'm really going to do this.* He couldn't believe his own nerve. Those other guys hadn't heard the voice mewling from the well. In fact, they thought he was crazy, and sometimes he wondered if they weren't right. But he'd heard it alright.

For the last week or so now, the voice from the well had been calling him. Well, to say it had been calling him was a not quite right, was it? It sort of emanated from the well, but he had heard it inside his head. Chris wasn't the youngest of them. At almost 11 years old, he had a hard time explaining the voice to the other boys, and he almost decked Danny when he laughed at him. But he figured that even a grown-up would have had a hard time describing the way the voice spoke to him. All he knew for sure was this; it was creepy. The call wavered into his head distant and crackly like something from one of those late night movies he liked to watch when his parents were already asleep; the black and white ones from the fifties and sixties.

Nearby, Mike nudged the football with his toe. It would have left a smeary trench in the new, soft snow, but the six of them had trampled most of it flat. Tom picked up the ball at his friend's foot and, without a word, the two of them returned to the yard and started tossing it back and forth.

"Danny. You're gonna keep that flashlight shining down in here, right?" Chris asked.

The other boy nodded.

"I can't hear you," Chris sang in a voice like a drill sergeant.

"Yeah, Chris. I'll shine the light in the well," Danny replied, obviously irritated.

"Good."

"You sure about this?" Derrick asked. "What if you fall?"

Chris glared at Derrick in disbelief. “You guys are gonna make sure I don’t, aren’t you?” he sneered.

The twins, Derrick and Darren, glanced at each other, some secret message flashing between them.

“Now, I want all of you over here, letting the line out slowly so I don’t drop like a stone,” Chris said. Then, just for good measure, he added, “And don’t do anything funny or I’ll kick each of your butts when I get back up here.”

Tom and Mike dropped the ball in the yard and sauntered back to where the others were already huddled around Chris and the well.

When all of the boys had a good grip on the rope, Chris squirmed into a repeller’s posture. If the well had been a little bit narrower, he might have been able to “walk” down with his back against one wall and his feet on the far side, but the opening was too wide for that. So he gave the command and four of the other boys let the rope out while Danny shined the flashlight into the hole.

Chris’ heart was pounding so hard he could hear the blood rushing in his ears. There was no telling what could be down there. The ancient shaft bore straight down without any visible obstacles or interruptions.

Maybe ten minutes later, his heart skipped a few beats when his foot slipped into thin air. The wall should have been there, but maybe a few stones had fallen loose. The boys above had let out most of the 100 foot rope. Still, the water gurgling at the bottom sounded like it was a mile below.

“Hold on. STOP!” He yelled at the others. The rope stopped its descent. He probed at the gap in the wall with his foot, but he could not feel the edges of the cavity.

“Hey. Gimme another foot,” he called. The rope obeyed, letting him down a little lower.

Now, he kicked his foot around in the opening, and he still couldn't feel any obstacle. It seemed to open up into a larger hole, maybe even a cave of some sort. Danny's flashlight offered little in the way of useable light down here. Chris wanted to take out his own and shine it into the void, but he needed both hands on the rope to keep the line from digging painfully into his armpits. He yelled more directions to the others.

"Alright. Let me down slowly until I say *stop*, okay?"

No one answered, but again, the line played out an inch at a time. When he passed the point where his feet could still touch the wall, they swung out behind him, leaving him to dangle at the end of the line. He wondered if this was what a worm felt like, dangling on the end of a line swinging around in a dark and alien world. When his feet found the wall again, he called for them to stop. He kicked out and swung back. On the return trip, his body should have slammed into the wall, but of course, it wasn't there. Instead, he swung onto some kind of landing where his feet found solid ground. When he stood up, he hit his head on the rocks above. The pain was exquisite, and he felt a bit dizzy, but at least the rope had relaxed. He slipped it over his head and let the looped end lie on the ground. Between his stinging armpits and his aching ribs, hanging from a rope that hooked under his arms had proven to be very uncomfortable. He didn't much look forward to the return trip.

When the dizzy spell passed and he was sure he wasn't going to fall from his ledge, Chris took the flashlight from his pack and fumbled for the switch. In the darkness, the thin beam was bright and made him squint. To his wonder, he found that this was not a cave at all. He had not known what to expect when he began this little journey, but somehow he was not shocked to find a tunnel cut deep into the bedrock wall of the well.

He wasn't sure what to do. Should he have one of the others join him? Maybe Danny. Sure, Danny would do it. Besides, he could really use someone to come down here and carry his pack. It was going to get heavy.

He called up to the other boys. "Danny. I need you to come down here. There's a tunnel."

One of the other boys, it sounded like Mike, answered back. "Are you safe down there?"

"What?" Chris yelled.

"Are you safe? You're not going to fall, are you?" Mike called again.

"Yeah. I'm fine. It's... There's a tunnel down here. Have Danny get his lazy butt down here."

The next voice to answer sounded like Tom. "I don't think so, Chris. I think we've had about enough of your crap."

"What are you talking about?" Chris yelled. But he already knew what they were talking about, didn't he? He had pushed too hard; been too cruel to them for too long. And he knew even before he heard the whispery sound of the rope skipping off the walls that he would not be returning home via the top of the well. Not today. Maybe not at all.

"Goodbye, Chris," one of the twins called.

"Yeah. Good luck," said his brother.

Then the hint of light from Danny's flashlight winked out and Chris started screaming. "No. Wait. Come back. I'm sorry. Tom, where are you?"

"Darren, Derrick? ... Come on, guys. This isn't funny." He waited for an answer, but none came.

"Danny? Please. ... Help me out of here."

In desperation, he screamed one last plea to Mike, begging him to drop another rope down into the well; then he just wept.

He probably sat there for an hour, maybe more, willing the rope to come back. He thought about those morons he hung around with and schemed his revenge. When they finally came back to let him out, they would pay. Oh yes, they would pay dearly. It never occurred to him that they might not ever come back.

Time marched on, and other thoughts began to assert themselves. First of all, he had played his flashlight all around himself, and there was another tunnel across the well. It must have been long because it just swallowed up his tiny light beam. His tunnel, as he had now begun to think of it, looked like it went a short distance and intersected with another. Most interesting of all was the way the walls almost appeared to be machined. The floor, the walls and the ceiling were nearly perfect in their straight machined edges and corners. It was like a mine tunnel carved by master stone cutters. But they must have been short; the ceiling wasn't more than four feet from the floor.

The other thing that gnawed at him was hunger. Four granola bars and a water bottle weren't going to last long. And if he was right about the voice in his head, then one of these tunnels must go somewhere. He decided he had to start exploring. He had no intention of jumping across the well opening to investigate the tunnel on the far side, so he turned and moved into the one behind him. It was not until he reached the intersection that he even remembered the orange spray paint can, which he dug out of his pack and used to mark the way he had come. He sprayed a simple "CP" and an arrow on the ceiling and then decided to go left. It was slow going, and crouching in the low tube made his back ache. Without warning, his flashlight began to flicker and dim. Now, for the first time, he began to feel real fear.

Batteries! He thought. *Why didn't I bring extra batteries?*

Several yards ahead, he thought he saw something moving. Not an animal. It was more like the tunnel itself was alive, but, of course, that was ridiculous. But his light was fading and his fear bloomed into sheer terror. There were two ways to go; forward or back. Neither seemed like a good option. He continued inching forward. Just as his flashlight began to illuminate a swirling mist before him, it went completely black. Chris whimpered quietly and continued, feeling his way along the smooth rock wall.

When he reached the place where he assumed the mist had been, the wall under his fingers changed. It started to feel warm and pleasant, even friendly. His terror shrank to fear, from fear to mild anxiety, to calm, to peace. A soothing feeling coursed through him. He didn't know where he was going, but as he slipped all the way into the mist, it occurred to him that he didn't really care.

CHAPTER 1

The Last Night on the Road

TEN YEARS AFTER Christopher's betrayal, another young man hurtled miserably toward his own destiny. For now, his face was dry, but Jeremiah Duncan McAllister had been crying for the better part of the last three days. He usually enjoyed his time with Aunt Marie, but she just didn't understand. Sometimes when he was really sobbing, she would try to tell him that he would make new friends, or that everything was going to be all right. Jerry knew that everything was *not* going to be all right! His world had just ended. He was leaving behind the school where he had started to feel like he fit in a little bit, a house that felt somewhat like a home, and the small group kids that he could almost call friends. The idea of leaving made him so upset that at times he almost felt like throwing up.

He was an average kid. He wasn't the tallest boy in his class, but was not short by any measure. His light brown hair turned almost blonde in late summer. He didn't like shirts with pictures of cartoon characters or sports figures, but went in for solid color t-shirts most of the time. As the weather had started to chill, he opted for rugby shirts to throw on over the tees. His favorite one, which he wore now, was alternating navy blue and forest green stripes, and it was as heavy as a blanket.

Jerry's life had finally started to take the shape that he had imagined it should. He had become friendly with some of the neighborhood kids and he had one good friend that he could share anything with. That was Kyle. Jerry could be himself around Kyle. He didn't have to pretend to care about professional sports or monster trucks. He and Kyle liked to launch their mountain bikes off dirt mounds. One nasty crash left him with a flat tire, and Kyle was there to help him repair it. Kyle had kept Jerry's secret about how he thought Melissa Rockhill was the most beautiful girl in Montclair Elementary School. Sometimes, they camped out together in a tent in Jerry's backyard. And on Saturdays in the summer, they had been allowed to ride their bikes together down to Jake's 24-7 Mini Mart almost a mile away to spend their allowance on candy or ice cream or comic books. All that was over... again. It always had to end again sometime.

He had never lived anywhere more than a year or two. In fact, in his ten years on this planet, Chester County, Pennsylvania, would be the eighth place he called home. His dad always seemed to find another job somewhere. It was always the same. "This will be the best thing for all of us, Jerry; the hospitals in Philadelphia are better suited to meet Becca's medical needs, Jerry; think of all the new friends you're going to make, Jerry." They always tried to make it sound so appealing, yet it always seemed to be more dismal than the time before.

His aunt's old Pontiac was a big car, but he was afforded a terribly small part of the back seat to call his own. There were suitcases and blankets piled almost to the ceiling alongside him in the back seat. He had a stuffed rabbit that traveled with him and a backpack with his CDs, some comic books, some drawing paper and a few action figures. He hardly opened the pack. He enjoyed drawing quite a bit and was really a talented artist for someone his age. He loved to draw creatures that he had seen in the comics. Most of them were hideous monsters, bulging with scar-pocked muscles and sharp teeth dripping with blood. He always felt bad for them. In the beginning of the stories, these beasts would destroy things and hurt people, but so often they turned out to be the misunderstood victims in the end. As the stories unfolded, they were revealed to be persecuted and tortured creatures. The *people* in the comic books that seemed to be the victims so frequently turned out to be the real monsters. Tonight he felt misunderstood and unwanted. In his mind, the monsters were the adults in his life; and *he* was certainly the victim.

Aunt Marie's Border collie was along for the ride, and the dog had more room than Jerry. That was because Molly had a dog bed to sleep in and curled up for hours on end. When Molly whined at the window, they would pull over at the nearest exit so that the animal would not mess up the car. Jerry had to pray for rest stops. When it wasn't raining, those rest stops were the only moments of relief that he had. Marie brought a Frisbee, and Jerry would play with the dog. Molly was a great Frisbee dog, as most Border collies are. When Jerry tossed it just right, she would pick it right out of the air, like a falcon on a sparrow, and bring it back to him. It was a blast, but it would have been more fun in his own backyard. The dread of having to return to the cramped car cast a dark cloud over any sunshine that seeped into his miserable existence.

On the road, the scenery was all different, but it was all the same. Trees, hills, businesses, houses and a whole lot of highway rolled out in front of them toward the ever receding horizon. It all looked foreign and hostile to Jerry. At night, the reflective 'cat's eyes' in the pavement ticked off countless miles in the trip like the second hand on a watch. Headlights from the other cars continuously drifted across the ceiling of the old car, reminding him of how alone he felt in the vast universe.

A firefly hit the windshield, leaving an inch long glowing smear on the glass. It made his stomach turn sour to think of the life that had just been snuffed out like a candle in a storm. His mom had always said that when he grew up, he would make an excellent entomologist because he was so fascinated with bugs, but he just could not bear the idea of having to work around all those dead insects nailed down to boards.

Jerry had always believed that all life, not just human life, was sacred. He did not feel that in God's eyes he was any more important than any other creature, be it a snake or a horse or a snail. Feeling kinship with all animals, it was not unusual for normally wild animals to approach him as if they were tame. And he almost always felt that on some unexplainable level he could sense their oneness, like they shared the same spirit.

After a couple hours on the Pennsylvania Turnpike, they exited onto a twisty back road in the middle of who-knew-where. The road seemed almost totally deserted. They had passed only one oncoming car in the past ten minutes. The only other signs of life came from the lights burning in the occasional homes they passed.

Without knowing where it came from, Jerry found himself suddenly anxious. There was no reason he could imagine to feel scared or nervous. Or was there? A misty image started to take shape in his mind's eye. Even as it came into focus, it wasn't exactly a clear picture like a photograph or a movie. This was more like a dream, kind of swimmy around the edges, but without that quality of unreality that can only come from a dream.

As it became clearer, he saw a twisty road in the night that looked a lot like this road, exactly like this road, in fact. Even having never been here before, he knew that it *was* this road. There were skid marks on the asphalt, fresh skid marks, broken and twisted. In his vision, and yes this was most definitely a vision, Jerry was shown dark liquid smears on the cool night pavement. And there was a car on the shoulder. Yes. There it was. It was dirty white with that fake wood on the doors. It was upside down on the roadside and the roof was squashed, but not quite flat against the passenger compartment. It had been a station wagon, Marie's station wagon! But it wasn't at rest yet. Marie's car was stopped in mid roll as if someone had pushed pause on the DVD player in the middle of the accident scene. It was perched on its nose and the roof was not actually on the ground. He could smell gasoline and see the electrical sparks under the hood where the battery must be shorting out against the frame of the car. A cloud of dust lingered in the air. And, oh, the screaming. If the person with the DVD remote had pushed pause, why could he still hear the screaming? He could hear it like he was actually there. It was two parts terror, one part pain. He was shown these things in frozen time. Nothing moved, and he could have wandered though the scene as long as he wished, looking at each detail, investigating it from every angle.

Then he noticed one of the tires, no all of them started to spin slowly, then faster. Time thawed quickly and things began to flow. The car completed its roll and the screaming abruptly stopped as the car slammed back down its roof again, this time mashing flat against the car's body panels. Even as the screaming had been silenced, he could not tune out the slow motion sound of twisting metal and breaking glass. He could see the deformed carcass of a large creature squash out from under the front of the car, and heard the sickening squish, crack, splock of its body being ravaged by the 4000 pound projectile. It occurred to him that this poor creature was the source of the black and glistening smears in the road.

There had been only one working headlight that swiped through the night. The headlight and remaining parking lights winked out at once as the car came to rest. Movement on the other side of the car caught his attention. He couldn't see it, but was acutely aware of the sound. Something was crashing through the woods. Coming at him? No. Running away! But not a person. It was bouncing, even, springing away.

"Marie. Slow down!" Jerry heard himself yell from the back seat. His vision had shown him one of his possible futures. Now he was back on real time.

"What?" She answered in a startled voice. She had already taken her foot off the gas.

"You have to slow down. There's something around the next corner!"

"Jerry, I am not..."

"Just do it, NOW!" he yelled.

Something in his panic must have made Marie brake. She was still approaching a curve, but she could not have believed that there was really something there. Rounding the sharp bend in the road at a significantly slower speed than they had been traveling a moment ago, the headlights lit up small herd of white tail deer. They froze the instant that her high beams washed over them. In slow motion, Jerry saw the faces of the helpless animals awaiting their fates like suspects in some twisted legal trial. It seemed like forever before Marie started to set the brakes, and they had traveled so much farther that he doubted that they would be able to stop in time. A yelp from Molly indicated that the dog had been wrenched from her bed and had most likely been thrown into the dashboard. The tires screamed out in defiance, wanting to continue rolling, but they had been forced to stop turning and began a sickening slide across the cool night pavement. The skid towards the powerless creatures was agonizingly slow to watch from the back seat. In this dreamlike state, many things occurred to Jerry, most of which were anger based. "Why wouldn't she listen to me?" he thought. "I told her to slow down, but nobody ever listens to me."

The car came to a jerky stop and bounced back, bobbing a couple times. It came to rest inches away from the closest deer. The deer stood motionless for another second or two. Then one of the group turned away from the lights and bounded into the woods. Another followed, and then the rest jumped away into the night, leaving Marie and Jerry alone in the car with a shaky dog. Marie took a couple deep breaths, and finally took her foot off the brake pedal. She let the car coast a short distance until there was a safe place to park on the shoulder.

At last, she turned to look at the boy in the back seat. "How did you know that?" She asked. Her expression showed a mix of suspicion and fear.

"I didn't know anything," Jerry lied. He was afraid that she would think he was some kind of freak if he told her the whole truth. Maybe he was. He had experienced a few of these premonitions before, but never so clearly that he knew with such certainty what the outcome would be. "I just got a little scared because I felt like we were going too fast on these twisty roads."

"But you said there was something around the corner," Marie responded, still breathing heavy.

"Yeah... I guess I did. But I was scared. I didn't really know what else to say. I just wanted you to slow down." The fact was that he had been really scared, but not just because she had been driving too fast for the road they were on. He had seen what was about to happen. He had seen the future!

Turning slowly back to the road, Marie seemed very suspicious of Jerry's explanation. She continued to watch him in the rear view mirror as if she might catch him doing something. What that might be, he could not imagine. He could only guess that she would not have believed the whole truth any easier. He also hoped she would not bring it up again later, especially around his mom. She would not let it drop so easily.

A few minutes later, they stopped at the third roadside motel of the trip. It was rundown and just looked uncared for. The old wooden sign read Happy Travelers Motor Lodge and below that in red neon letters, the word vacancy shone like a garish, red beacon in the night. Upon entering the frigid room, Jerry headed to the bathroom. When he switched on the bathroom light, two or three large black insects scurried across the floor and under the toilet. This sight caused a queasy feeling to churn about in the pit of his stomach. The carpets had used chewing gum smashed into them and what appeared to be old soda stains. He kept his shoes and socks on.

The pictures on the walls looked like they had been there for a hundred years. Faded and dingy, the country landscapes depicted a type of barn that Jerry had never seen before; ancient structures built into hillsides, with second floors supported on one side by several heavy timbers propped on top of squatty columns of stone. Both prints were winter scenes, which didn't make Jerry feel any warmer.

"I know it's a little dumpy Jer, but it was the only place out here that would accept pets," Marie told him, still eyeing him warily after the premonition incident.

Jerry didn't say anything, but his twisted face spoke loud enough. The musty odor of a damp basement permeated everything. The pool outside was gated off and closed for the season. That suited Jerry just fine. Even if it had been warm enough to put his suit on, there were piles of leaves and sticks in the corners of the chain link fence surrounding it. A couple of the white plastic chairs lay half submerged where no one had bothered to retrieve them after the last storm.

Outside many of the rooms, black metal boxes with holes in the sides alerted visitors to the fact that the place also had a rodent problem. *Big surprise,* thought Jerry.

Aunt Marie ordered a medium pizza and a two-liter root beer for them to share. At least the hotel they had stayed in the night before had cable. This TV picked up four channels, and two of them were so fuzzy that they didn't even count. Jerry pulled his CD player out and put on some music while he pretended to read a comic.

When the food arrived, the pizza was cold and the soda was warm. The delivery guy didn't bring any plates so they had to use napkins. It was almost more than he could take. They each sat on their own beds and stared at the TV, neither of them really watching what was on, while they mindlessly chewed on cold, soggy pizza.

"When do you think we will get to the new house?" Jerry finally asked.

Marie broke her connection with the TV to look at her nephew and answered, "Probably around lunchtime tomorrow. I have to call your mom when we're done eating." She took another bite of her food, then asked, "Do you want to talk to her?"

He didn't answer for a moment, but then resentfully he said, "Yeah, I guess so." He was trying really hard to hold on to the anger he felt towards his mom. She had let his dad sell the house, which in his mind made her just as responsible as his dad for this whole relocation thing. He was trying to stay mad, but he missed her all the same.

Clean up after dinner was easy. They just tossed the napkins and cups into the almost empty pizza box and dropped it beside the trashcan. Marie fished her cell phone from her purse and dialed.

"Sarah? Hi," he heard her say into the phone. He could hear the buzz of what must have been his mom's voice talking back, but it was inaudible.

"Yeah," Marie said. "Jeremiah and I had another quiet day. It rained most of the way from Columbus to the Pennsylvania border, but it cleared up before we got on the turnpike. He seems kinda distant; really takin' it hard. And he's still crying a lot." There was another pause while his mom answered back, then, "Sure. He's right here."

Jerry took the phone from his aunt. "Hi. Mom?"

"How ya doin', Punkin?" she asked him. He really didn't care much for the nickname but they had an understanding; she was only ever to use it around family.

"I'm kinda tired from all the riding," he said. "It's real cramped in the back seat, and I'm pretty bored."

"Well, it shouldn't be too much longer, honey. Marie says you only have few hours of driving left in the morning."

Aunt Marie leashed up Molly and signaled that she was going to take her out for a walk. She pulled on her coat, opened the door and strode out into the dark parking lot. A crisp wave of cold, November air rolled across the floor and Jerry pulled his dangling feet back up onto the bed. He wanted to take advantage of being alone and tell his mom how gross the room was, but he held back the complaints. His mom would just overreact and then there would be a heated discussion between the two sisters. He figured his mom had enough to worry about without his petty concerns adding to it.

"Yeah. I will really be glad to get out of the car and sleep in my own bed tomorrow night," he said.

"It's all set up," she replied. "We paid one of the movers a little extra to hang around for an extra day and help set some of the stuff up. He put your shelves together and helped me move some of the furniture around. We are still up to our necks in moving boxes, so it could take months for us to dig out."

Jerry knew that his mom would never let that happen. Those boxes would be unpacked and recycled within the next two weeks. "Did you unpack my comics or my nature books?" he asked her, concerned that she might have thrown out some of the comics she didn't quite approve of. Besides an admirable comic book collection, his assortment of nature books was also extensive, and they were not just picture books. Many of the nature handbooks were field guides written to appeal to botanists and zoologists alike. He still held on to a few of his dinosaur books from when he was a younger kid, but his interest in nature had shifted away from the extinct. He now favored learning about endangered species. In this changing world, he deeply wished to know what he could do to help the beasts that could not defend themselves against the ever-encroaching destruction brought on by mankind. In fact, when he was only seven years old, he had chosen, with his parents' blessing, to stop eating any meat. It just made him gag to think that what he was eating had once been one of God's living, breathing creatures. That lasted almost a year, but even now he didn't eat much 'animal flesh'.

"No. I promised that I would leave that box for you. Most of your other stuff is already unpacked. I put your models on the top two shelves and the videos in your TV stand. The cable hasn't been hooked up yet, but they are supposed to be out on Friday."

Jerry could tell that she was just trying to cheer him up. He somehow sensed that she thought she might feel a little less guilty if she could make him feel better. He didn't want it to be that easy for her.

"I really miss Kyle," he said almost crying. "He said he was going to write. Did I get any mail yet?" he asked.

"Nothing yet, Honey. It's only been three days, but I'll shake down the mailman for you if he gets here before you do tomorrow. I miss you, Punkin'. I can't wait to see you." His mom sounded misty, and as if on cue, Aunt Marie and Molly tromped back into the room.

Jerry handed the phone back to his aunt and got his pajamas from the suitcase. Disgusted by the conditions of the room, he kept his socks on so that he would not have to walk barefoot on the carpet. He wanted to put his shoes on just to go brush his teeth. Since his aunt wasn't paying him any attention anyway, he skipped his teeth today. He wasn't sure that his toothpaste was going to be strong enough to kill any germs that might flow from the faucet in the room anyway, and his water bottle was out in the car.

He crawled under his covers. The bed sagged in the center like a giant bowl and, smack-dab in the middle of the mattress, a spring pushed up against him. The sheets felt almost as grungy as the carpet. Marie finished up her end of the day ritual and headed for her bed where Molly waited with her head lying across her own back feet. His aunt took out an atlas and plotted the coming day's route, then said, "Good night." She switched off the light and pulled the covers up on her bed.

The room was dark, almost black. A ray of light pierced the room through a crack in the curtains. It shot across the beds like a laser, but it didn't offer enough light to quiet Jerry's imagination.

In the hushed darkness, he could hear several voices coming from a few rooms away. It sounded like there were dozens of people there, but he was sure it was only a few teenagers. He had only been in bed a few minutes when he heard a bottle break, followed by some excited yelling. It sounded like they were cheering over something; maybe a basketball game. Molly picked up her head and looked toward the window, but lay back down after a moment or so. Marie mumbled something that sounded like she was swearing, but he couldn't be sure. It made him nervous. He could not feel safe with all the noise. He tried to ignore it and go to sleep, but then he heard an adult yelling at the teens to quiet down or get out. There was a slamming door and then it got really quiet.

In this new silence, he started to think he could hear noises in his room. He remembered the bugs in the bathroom and could picture them crawling around in his bed. He tried to think about something else. He thought about being back at his old house. Down the street, there was a lot of construction on new houses. In the dirt, there were trails with dips and jumps, and he loved launching his bike off of the homemade ramps and trying to do stunts and tricks with it. This activity sent him to the hospital a couple times to be sewn back together, but he would always try it again. On his bike, there was a sense that he was in control for a while. Now, he could hear his aunt's snoring, and he just felt horribly alone again. He lay there for hours before finally falling off into a fitful sleep.

His dreams were filled with mazes of underground tunnels. He couldn't see his feet through the fog on the floor and the ceiling wasn't visible either, but he could feel it. In the walls of many of the caves there were rocks that pulsed with a dim yellow light, making the entire environment appear to be alive.

Down here he met some small human-like creatures. They looked like elves or leprechauns, but they didn't dress like that at all. Instead, they wore something similar to army fatigues, but the camouflage pattern was black and yellow, and no pointed hats. With tousled hair and mangy beards, they gave him the impression of men who had been on a mission that left them no time for rest or self-care. There were other creatures too. Some resembled big rats, about two feet tall that dressed in deep royal blue jackets and black trousers. Their sleeves were covered with pins and badges. There were 6-legged lizards with huge white eyes that spoke in a different language, but he understood everything they said. They had skin tones that matched their surroundings, and they walked on only their two back legs, leaving the rest of their appendages free to manipulate their tools and weapons with amazing dexterity. This community of characters got along together exceptionally well, although they didn't intermingle with each other a great deal.

And he could sense something else too; pain. Not his own pain, but there was almost a physical presence of fear and dread that pushed in at the edges of his dreams.

CHAPTER 2

The New House

WHEN JERRY WOKE in the morning, he was disoriented. The room was unfamiliar and it took a few minutes for him to realize where he was, who he was with and why he was there. As reality sank in, so did a bit of the previous night's dream. It was really hazy, but it left him with a feeling of inexplicable, yet very real dread. The images of the tunnels and their inhabitants were not available to Jerry's consciousness. The only clear picture that followed him into the daylight was an old well.

This was a "Jack and Jill" style well with the stone ring and a little roof over it. The timbers that supported the roof had a cross member that would have supported a pulley for a bucket on a rope. The well shaft looked as if it went straight to the center of the earth. He could see a short distance into it, but it quickly turned black. There was snow on the slate roof and on the edges of the stone ring that formed the top of the well shaft, but the snow was mostly brushed away. On the ground, footprints were everywhere. They crossed and tracked over each other in so many directions that Jerry got the impression there had been a struggle by the well.

"Wow! You slept late." Marie's voice brought him all the way back to the real world. The dreams were gone and he was back in that disgusting hotel room. He looked at the clock on the night-stand. It was 9:30 in the morning. "I didn't want to wake you but I was beginning to think I was going to have to. We have to check out by 11:00 and I thought you should have time for a shower before you head back to your mom."

"You could have woken me," Jerry replied. He noticed that she was already dressed. "You already had a shower? I didn't hear a thing."

"Yep. Took Molly out, too. It hasn't warmed up much from last night yet. You'll probably want to pick out a sweater for this morning," she answered.

"Man," Jerry thought. "How could she be so perky?"

Once he was dressed and ready to leave, Jerry dragged his overnight bag out to the car and stuffed it into the small space in the back from where he had removed it the night before. Marie and Molly followed him out. She had already warmed up the car, so they left their jackets in the back, quickly got into the car and pulled the doors closed. The doughnuts that they had eaten in the motel lobby had been dry and the milk not so cold. They were still hungry, so they drove through a fast food restaurant and got an early lunch.

With about three hours of driving ahead of them, Jerry slipped his headphones over his ears and got out his drawing pad. He opened it up to a blank page and started to doodle. He wasn't really drawing with a purpose, but as his sketch began to take form, he found himself drawing a creature he had never seen in any of his comics. It was a lizard-like animal, its skin mostly black with a scaly but smooth texture. It had six legs, or more accurately, two legs and four arms. Six long thin fingers or toes completed the hands and feet. There were no claws or fingernails, but each of the tiny appendages was capped off with a slightly bulbous tip. The creature stood on its two back legs and balanced with his tail. In its right two arms, it held a shovel like tool, but instead of a traditional spade-shaped head, the tip of the shovel had two rounded points. In its other hands, the creature clung to a bizarre weapon. It resembled a ray gun from a 1950's sci-fi movie, but it was almost as long as the shovel, and there was no visible trigger. The business end was fitted with two small very polished, silver spikes that could have been bayonets. The barrel portion of the device was encapsulated in a coil. The animal was wearing a helmet embellished with a glowing, yellow stone on its crown and a spike on top. A sheet of chain mail hung from the back of the helmet to protect the creature's neck. The only other garment he wore was a piece of amour that covered his shoulders, back and chest. The armor's chest was smooth and contoured with overlapping plates that allowed that piece to move with the warrior within. The back-plate was studded with spikes that matched the one on the helmet. He had very large white eyes with no visible pupils. The nostrils were almost imperceptible, sitting on the flat bridge of a nose that ran above its entire mouth.

Jerry worked on his sketch for almost the entire trip to the new house. He never really remembered having seen a creature like this before, but he labored on it with the confidence of someone who was very familiar with his subject. And it was one of the most realistic drawings he could ever remember creating.

"Go ahead and start cleaning up," his aunt called from the front seat. "Looks like we'll be there in about five minutes."

He was almost finished filling in the background with his colored pencils. "Gimme just another minute. I'm almost done." He glanced out the window for the first time. All he could see were trees. Not pine trees like the ones that grew at his old house in Minnesota; these were almost all leafy, deciduous trees. There were some houses mixed in, mostly set way back off of the road, and many of them were built of stone. He was used to seeing homes covered with wood or vinyl siding. Without finishing his picture, he decided to pack up anyway.

One house that caught his eye was built of stone with a slate roof. It was two stories tall with white trim around all the windows. There were so many windows. The driveway snaked up to the house and separate three-car garage through sparse trees. Two of the garage doors were opened to reveal a very expensive looking car and what might have been another car under a big green tarp. The yard around it was immaculately maintained with flowerbeds by the front door and trees scattered throughout. Mounted onto a permanently fixed pole by the side of the driveway was a regulation basketball hoop. There was playground equipment in the backyard that would leave many small city parks envious. It was beautiful, and Jerry found himself imagining what kind of life those people must live. Did they throw big parties and entertain important people? Maybe the children who lived there went to private boarding schools and were out of the state, or even the country right now. He could only imagine, because this was not the life that he lived.

They turned onto a short street with no outlet and a cul-de-sac at the end. Marie announced that this was the place. There were only seven homes here on Lakeview Court, but right away, Jerry decided that the name didn't fit. He didn't see a lake anywhere. The houses were all built of stone and had medium sized front lawns. The trees were mostly stripped away from the fronts of them leaving only a few bare carcasses scattered about their yards. Two of the homes had big wooden swing sets in the yards, so Jerry assumed that there were at least some kids in the neighborhood. To anyone else, the little street would have had a peaceful and serene feel to it. To Jerry, it just felt depressing.

The sky had clouded up over the last hour or so and a few snowflakes floated gently to the ground. Marie pulled into the third house on the right and switched off the car. It was almost at the end of the street. It was the only house on the block with no trees in the front yard. The house had only three windows upstairs. There were no curtains in them yet, but Jerry knew that would be fixed soon. Downstairs there was a front door at the center of the house with larger windows flanking it on either side. The door and shutters were all pale blue and the mailbox was painted to match. Attached to the house on the right side was a two-car garage. There was a pile of spent moving boxes and some other trash by the street. He thought he could have made a great fort with them inside, but there was no way he was going to be seen bringing them back into the house. He didn't want anyone to get the idea that he still enjoyed doing those 'little-kid' things.

Before they were out of the car, his mom opened the front door and graciously swept out to welcome them.

"We really missed you, Punkin." Hugging him, his mom nodded her head in the direction of the house. Jerry looked over and saw his sister smiling at them from inside the door. His mom and sister had come out almost a week ahead of him to try to prepare for the movers and to start unpacking. Becca wasn't much help as she was only seven and confined to a wheelchair, but his mom liked having her around. "Hope you had a nice ride today." Then to Marie she said, "Come on in. I made a homemade chicken potpie this morning. I'll help you unload after you've had a chance to rest up a bit."

Jerry pulled his backpack from the car, carried it across the short sidewalk and up the three steps to the front door. He was looking forward to a little comfort food after all the fast food he had been eating. His mom and aunt were right behind him as he reached the door. He pulled the glass door open and stepped into the new place. The floors were all a light colored hardwood. The walls were painted in pale tan and the tall white molding gave the inside a dramatic, rich look. To the right, a staircase climbed up to the next floor. Jerry started to climb the stairs to try to find his room, but his mom asked him to wait. "First we'll eat some lunch and then I'll show you around," she said in that voice she saved for when she really didn't want much discussion on the subject.

Jerry's mom had already set the table. She had out the linen napkins and the good china. He had been using expensive silverware as long as he could remember, so the heavy feel of it just reminded him more of his old home. Mom and Aunt Marie talked about the neighborhood and a little bit about the cultural advantages of being so close to Philadelphia. There was always a show downtown, and the people were far more sophisticated than the backwoods folks they used to live near. Jerry never saw anything different about the people back in Minnesota. True, there had not been a big city within a four hours drive, but the Internet brought a world of shopping and news right to their doorstep.

"They make a cheese steak sandwich down at a place called Tony's that is to die for. They use the best rolls, soft on the inside and crusty on the outside." his mom said. "Those subs that you could get at the gas station by the lake just never really did much for me." Marie looked like she was ready to trade in her chicken pie for one of Tony's cheesesteaks.

After lunch, Jerry convinced his mom to leave the dishes on the counter and get on with the tour. Starting from the kitchen, she showed them the basic layout of the first floor and where the basement was. In the front corner of the house on the end opposite the garage was Rebecca's bedroom. In the last house they had installed a device that would carry her up the stairs, but his parents decided that a ground floor room would make her life much easier. As they came around to the back door, Jerry stepped out onto the deck to admire the woods behind the house. He looked forward to hiking up the hill at the back of the yard and into the forest. There were a few scattered trees on the yard itself as well as a small stand of rhododendrons near the back corner.

The next leg of the tour took them upstairs to the rest of the bedrooms. The room to the right was his mom's 'creative' room. This room housed her sewing machine, fabric, fabric paints, baskets, colored paper and other craft supplies. It was a small room and looked out into the woods behind the house. Straight off the top of the stairs was a room that, once unpacked, would be the guest bedroom. At the end of the short hall was his parent's room.

As he rounded the top of the staircase to the left, Jerry found his own room. He and his mom and Aunt Marie looked into it for a moment. Jerry felt mixed up. He loved being near his things again, but he still ached for Minnesota. The sight of the Lego's on the shelf instantly took him back in his mind to all the afternoons he had spent building imaginary worlds with Kyle. He started getting a little misty, as if he were about to start crying again. His aunt must have seen this.

"Sarah, I'm going to straighten up the kitchen a bit," Marie said. With that, she turned and left the two of them alone in Jerry's doorway.

After what seemed to Jerry like hours, his mom said, "I know it's hard Honey. We all liked the old neighborhood. Your dad and I had friends there too, you know? ...And so did Becca. It's not going to be easy on her either."

This statement just made him surge with rage. "Then why did you bring us here? Huh? How come you made us leave somewhere we loved if it's going to be so tough on Becca? Everything is always about her! Ever since she first..."

His mother cut him off. "THAT'S ENOUGH! You know that it is not a choice whether to take care of her or not." She continued in a hushed, but stern voice. "The choice we had to make was one of *how* to care for her. The 4-hour trip to Minneapolis was very difficult on all of us. Here we are only a half hour from the children's hospital. We won't have to take her out of school for two extra days each time she has an appointment with the specialists, and we can stay together as a family more often." Frequently, he and his dad would stay at home for a few days while his mom and Rebecca went to the hospital for tests or rehab consultations. He never felt like such a burden as when his dad would stay home from work to take care of him.

She continued to harp at him about how important it was for Becca and for his dad, and about how selfish he was being. He had stopped listening, and had gone to the happy place in his mind where he was the important one for a while. It was the place where his parents loved him unconditionally, and he was respected. When she finally left him to head back downstairs, he was relieved to be alone with his toys and his books. He scanned his room for the box; the one with the comics. As he opened the box of magazines, his troubling thoughts of unworthiness gave way to a world where he was a hero, a world where he had respect and he had total control of not only his own destiny, but the course of all human endeavors. As the afternoon wore on, Jerry unpacked that box one book at a time and placed them into their cataloged magazine cartons on his shelves.

At dinner, Jerry didn't speak at all. He was still angry about the whole exchange in his bedroom. His dad was still at work, and it looked like he may not even be home before Jerry went to bed. His mom explained that she had already made arrangements with the school district to have a handicapped school bus pick them both up in front of the house. He may not have been speaking, but this got his attention. He wanted to be like the other kids, to ride the real bus and try to blend in. There was no blending in when the bus full of kids makes a special stop to pick up a kid in a wheelchair. As bad as things looked before this, he was certain things were only about to get worse.

CHAPTER 3

Bear Run Elementary School

NO ONE SAID A WORD as Rebecca's wheelchair was raised up onto the bus that Thursday morning. Some of the kids were watching the lift pull the empty wheelchair up to the level of the bus' floor to be wheeled in. Most were gaping at the house with a look of deep interest. It looked as though they were expecting something to happen. His sister had already been placed in a seat beside her wheelchair, while Jerry and another girl who looked to be in kindergarten boarded the bus. As Jerry looked around for a seat, some of the other kids started to stare at him with obvious curiosity. He could only see two empty seats on the bus; one next to his sister, and one beside a friendly looking boy across the aisle form her. His sense of duty to family was weighing heavy and he felt like he *should* sit next to her, but he was still looking for someone to blame for the move to Pennsylvania. He sat down next to the kid across from her and tried hard not to make eye contact with anyone. The kid beside Jerry was a regular enough looking boy with short, straight, black hair, blue eyes and a confident air. In a navy blue t-shirt with a picture of a snow capped mountain and a collage of climbing gear, he looked like the rugged outdoor type.

Jerry could feel the stares from the other kids and hear the whispers as the bus bounced along the backwoods road. The driver seemed to be quite adept at guiding his vehicle into every possible pothole. Finally the boy next to him broke the silence.

"That's a pretty weird house," he said to Jerry. "Did you know that no one has lived there for over 10 years?"

Jerry was stunned. "What are you talking about?"

"That is your house, right? The one with the blue shutters?"

"Yeah," Jerry said slowly. "What do you mean no one has lived there for years?" His head was suddenly swimming. The house did not look like it had been abandoned to him. But why would this kid make up such a story. If it had been vacant for so long, why hadn't his mom told him?

A girl who looked about six or seven years old sitting behind him broke in, "Some kid died there. Fell down the well and never came back out."

The first kid continued, "They say he was playing football with a some of the other neighborhood kids and just fell in. His parents were so sad they just moved away. They tried to sell the house, but lots of people feel there's something too spooky about living in a house where there was such a tragedy. They're kinda superstitious about that stuff."

Then the girl said, "Bobby, tell him about the other kids, about how they all disappeared one at a time over the next few months."

The first kid, Bobby, continued, "Yeah. There were five other boys there that day. None of them really liked Chris very much. That's the kid's name who lived in your house, Christopher Pritchard. Anyway, he was kind of a bully. They say that sometimes kids would play with him just so that he wouldn't pick on them as much. Lots of other kids tried to get the details from these five guys and they would never talk about it. The grown ups always told us that they were just too upset to discuss it. Always seemed like such an exciting story to keep to yourself. Then, about three months later, the first kid vanished. "

Jerry was starting to become annoyed. He looked the kid beside him in the eyes and asked, "Are you kidding me? You expect me to believe that some kid died in a well in my yard, which by the way, there is no well, and that the house has been empty since then. Then all the other kids that were with him disappeared. Do I look like an idiot?" Jerry asked.

Rebecca jumped in to the conversation and said, "Jerry, there *is* an old fashioned well in the backyard."

"No there isn't."

"Yes there is. It's in those bushes in the back corner," Becca countered.

Jerry couldn't come up with anything to say. Part of him wished that the story might be true. This was just the kind of creepy story that 10 year old boys loved. But, no. Next they would be trying to tell him that his house was haunted. *The spirits of the lost boys still wander the house at night looking for a soul to take with them to the great beyond.* He wasn't buying what they were selling, but then again...

He had even less interest in going to school now. He was itching to investigate the backyard. Finally, to his sister, Jerry snapped, "How would you know anything about a well in the yard?"

Becca answered, "Mom wheeled me out in the yard the other day. Since there are no sidewalks, she pushed me around back to get a closer look at the trees. When we got almost to the woods, I saw it. I asked mom to take me over there, but she said it was off limits and showed me where our well is now. It just looks like a plastic pipe sticking out of the ground with a metal hat on top."

"Anyway," Bobby went on, "This isn't some kind of joke." An older red haired kid sitting in front of them shook his head. "After the first guy disappeared, no one suspected it had anything to do with Chris. But then the youngest one, a 4th grader turned up missing. Last place anyone saw him, he was headed into the woods with his dog. That night the dog came home, alone! Now there are only three left right; and it's a snow day. It's about three weeks later. Schools are closed and an ice storm has pulled down the power lines. All the parents are home from work. So kid number 3, Daniel Patterson went out to get some firewood; he was never heard from again. Finally, the last two boys' parents just can't stand it anymore and they moved out of town. They were brothers and lived in the house across the street from you, the one with the green swing set in the side yard."

Jerry was dumbfounded. There must have been some kind of conspiracy to play a really nasty trick on the new kid. Who would ever believe such a crazy story? The first part about the kid falling into the well was one thing, but they were describing his house as if it had a curse on it. No, Jerry wasn't falling for this story. He wasn't superstitious, and he definitely wasn't going to look stupid. "I don't believe a word of this!" he snapped. "What is this; pick on the new kid day? See what we can get him to believe?" He turned away from Bobby and the girl and just looked up front. Some of the other kids were looking back at him, but they weren't laughing. He looked away and tried to just watch out the front window. Slowly, however, he became aware that even the bus driver was staring at him. He just wanted to curl up and hide.

After a few minutes in the heavy and awkward silence, the girl behind Bobby spoke up again. "How come you need a wheelchair?" she inquired of Rebecca.

"Ashley! That's none of your business!" Bobby sounded shocked. She was obviously his little sister.

"No. That's Okay," said Rebecca. "When I was 5, I fell down the stairs and I broke two vertebrae in my neck. There was a bunch of nerve damage, and now my legs don't work right."

"Will you ever be able to walk again?" asked another kid sitting over her shoulder.

"Dunno," she answered. "Most of the doctors say that the way research is going, there is real hope for the future, but it's probably many years away."

Another little boy about two seats back put in, "Does it go real fast? It looks like it would be fun."

Rebecca turned around and told him mater-of-factly that it was fun sometimes, but mostly the wheel chair was a real nuisance. She talked about how she couldn't go up the stairs or change her own clothes. She talked about how people always looked like they felt sorry for her. And how sometimes, when people stared, she felt embarrassed. Jerry watched and listened as his sister stole the spotlight. Man, he hated how she always got all the attention. But today, that was okay. He just wanted to be alone with his thoughts. He didn't want to believe the stories, but his gut was telling him they were true.

When the bus got to school, most of the kids filed off. Jerry stayed behind with his sister. He helped her into her chair and they went into the building together. Rebecca's chair had a big pocket on the side where she could keep her lunch and her books. Jerry had an almost empty backpack on his shoulder. They found their way to the office where the school secretary asked them to wait while she paged Mr. Shumaker, the principal.

He was a tall man with glasses and what little hair he had over his ears was combed across the top of his head, which was otherwise completely bald. He wore a light blue button up shirt with a solid navy blue tie and navy blue dress pants. He wore brown, comfortable shoes. And he had an open, approachable demeanor, like he might even be someone's grandfather.

"Welcome to Bear Run Elementary," he said with a friendly voice. "You must be Jerry." He held out his hand and Jerry responded by reaching up to meet the obligatory handshake. "And you must be Rebecca. Your mother has told me a lot about you. We are really looking forward to having you both here this year. If you ever have any questions about the building or the people here, just come and see me any time." Jerry got the impression he really meant it.

Mr. Shumaker gestured towards the door, and the two children exited the office with the principal. He escorted them down the first hallway on the left to the third door on the right side. The door was open, since many of the students had not yet arrived. Stepping into the room, the principal called to the teacher, "Mrs. Kelso?"

A younger lady turned and smiled. "Hello, Mr. Shumaker. Is this our new student?"

"Yes it is," he replied. "This is Rebecca McAllister, and I know you will make her quite comfortable on her first day here." Some of the kids in the room were looking at the door to see the new girl, but most of the second graders were busy talking to each other or coloring and drawing.

"So I hear that you are from Minnesota," Mrs. Kelso said to Rebecca as she showed her into the classroom. Jerry could still hear Mrs. Kelso talking to her as Mr. Shumaker directed him further down the same hallway.

A few doors to the right, a short Asian man was standing on a footstool outside a classroom with the door open. He was tacking some papers up on a corkboard for display. When Jerry and Mr. Shumaker approached, the teacher stopped what he was doing and stepped down to the floor.

"Good morning, Mr. Hong," Mr. Shumaker said. "This is the new boy I told you about. He's going to be in your class."

"Good. Nice to meet you, Mr. McAllister," the teacher responded to Jerry. The man's accent surprised Jerry. He had been expecting a Chinese or Japanese accent, but there was no trace of anything like that. In fact, he sounded like a Midwesterner. "Mr. Shumaker tells me you are from Minnesota. I grew up just outside of St. Paul. What town are you from?"

As Mr. Hong placed the stack of papers he was holding onto the footstool, Jerry collected himself and answered, "Maple Lake. It's a small town a few hours from there." He instantly liked this man.

"How do you like Chester County so far?" Mr. Hong asked him.

"Its nice." he lied. His mind was overflowing with so many thoughts that he could not imagine trying to carry on a conversation.

Mr. Shumaker said, "Jerry. Your mother told me you might be interested in joining the ski club. Mr. Hong is the club coordinator."

"Do you like to ski?" Mr. Hong asked Jerry.

"I've never tried, but it looks like fun. Is it hard to learn?" He asked the teacher.

"I'm going to leave you guys," the principal said. Mr. Hong nodded.

"It takes a couple trips to really get the hang of it, but the worst part is getting all your gear on," Mr. Hong explained. "It's kinda like roller skating. Do you skate much?" Jerry assured him that he loved to skate, and couldn't wait for the first ski trip.

A few more kids filed past them, laughing and pushing each other. The teacher retrieved his papers from the footstool, and led Jerry into the classroom. Jerry followed him to the desk where Mr. Hong handed him a tan folder. A sticker with Jerry's personal information printed on it had been stuck on the top corner. "This is the school code of conduct and orientation handbook. You will need to review it with your parents. Then sign it and return it when you can. There is also some information about what I expect from my students and what they should be able to expect from me. I think you will find that we'll get along pretty well as long as you don't goof off *too* much." Jerry believed him. He seemed very sincere.

After the bell rang and the students found their seats, Mr. Hong made the announcement to the rest of the class that there was a new student. This moment always went poorly in the past. His last teacher introduced him as Jeremiah, and the class laughed mercilessly. The moment came, and the teacher introduced him as Jerry McAllister. Mr. Hong did not even ask him to come up front, but to just stand up for a moment. As he scanned the class for the rejection he anticipated, he noticed that Bobby, the kid from the bus, was sitting three rows over, and he was wearing a friendly smile. As the wave of terror slowly receded, he smiled back and sat down again.

The morning slipped by without incident, but he couldn't completely shake that first-day-as-the-new-kid anxiety. The last class before lunch was Library. The librarian, Mrs. Sheppard, was reviewing last week's lesson on periodicals. As she expanded her lesson today to include newspapers, she reminded the students that Mr. Hong expected them to write essays on an event that happened in Pennsylvania in the last 100 years. After spending about half of the period on lecture, she told the students to split into groups of two or three to go to the computers and hunt for information on the topics they had chosen weeks ago. This being Jerry's first day, he had no topic and had not been paired up with any other students yet. Anxious at the prospect of not finding a partner, he looked over at Bobby who nodded his head back to him, signaling that he could join his group.

When they were allowed to get up, Jerry made his way over to Bobby, who was joined by another boy that Jerry had not noticed before. He was a fair skinned African American kid with a friendly smile. His black hair was short and tightly curled against his head with the slightest hint of red-orange sprinkled in around the edges. He was skinny, and gave the impression of being a long distance runner or a basketball player. "This is CJ. He's a geek in training. Already built his first computer from parts he had his dad pick up at Computer Good Buys. He and I have been looking at some real interesting stuff for the last few weeks."

Uncomfortably, Jerry said, "Hello," and they all headed over to the last available computer. It was, of course, connected to the Internet and CJ sat down at the keyboard. Bobby and Jerry flanked him on either side as he typed 'Chris Pritchard, Chester County Eagle' into the search bar.

"Bobby tells me you moved into a pretty special house," CJ said to Jerry. He grinned knowingly at Bobby. CJ was obviously comfortable around a computer. There were several pages of results almost instantly from his Internet search. He clicked on the first one, and a news story opened up immediately with the headline *"Boy's Disappearance Ruled Accident."* For a moment Jerry forgot how to breathe. It *was* real. His heart was racing, and he was unaware of anything around him. After a short eternity, Jerry became vaguely aware that the other two boys were watching him intently.

"Dude, you alright?" Bobby asked him. CJ looked a little concerned too.

Jerry found his ability to talk again. "I... This really happened? I thought you might be, you know, having some fun with the new kid."

They both nodded at him, and his gaze returned to the article on the screen. There was a picture of a boy, about his age, with a troubled smile and a dark t-shirt. It was a black and white photo, so there was no way to see the color of his eyes or his shirt, but his hair was definitely black; jet black, as he had once heard someone say, although to the best of his knowledge, Jerry had never seen a black jet. He had a slender face with a smallish mouth and a nose that was almost lost on his face. His eyes were somewhat close together, but what caught Jerry was how those eyes appeared to be looking right into his very soul. Jerry was mesmerized. He felt like he was looking straight into the eyes of a long lost brother! It wasn't like he was looking at his identical twin in the physical sense. This was deeper. It was more like the boy in the photo was calling out to him as only a kindred spirit could. The caption under the picture read, *Christopher Pritchard, 10 year old son of Margaret and Randy Pritchard, remains missing two weeks after falling into the well in his backyard.* And though he had nothing to base it on, Jerry had the disquieting feeling that this Christopher Pritchard would play a bigger part in his future than just being the kid who died in his house.

CHAPTER 4

The Well

BOBBY AND CJ helped Jerry through the lunch line. Jerry picked up a square slice of pizza, a milk and a cup of vanilla pudding, but he was too dizzy to eat. He could not reconcile in his brain the fact that Christopher Pritchard was dead with the nagging feeling that he was very much alive.

"So what were my parents thinking?" Jerry said out loud, although mostly to himself. Then to Bobby, "Do you think maybe they don't know?"

CJ answered, "They *must* know about it. I think realtors are supposed to tell you about things like that."

"So why would you buy a house like that? A lot of people would think it was cursed or something. I mean, someone died there, right? And then there's all that stuff about the other guys. This is just weird." Jerry wasn't used to having someone he could talk to at lunch. In Maple Lake, each class ate at it's own table, and Kyle was in a different class. Before he saw the article for himself, he was suspicious about Bobby's and CJ's motives, but they seemed sincerely interested in him. A lot of kids were staring at him and whispering and it made him a bit uncomfortable, but he just focused more on the conversations with his new friends.

Bobby was first to respond. “Maybe they didn’t think that it was a big deal. Grownups don’t always seem to know what’s really important.”

“...or maybe they thought you might not find out,” retorted CJ.

Bobby laughed loudly at this idea. “You have got to be kidding me! That house is legend. Everyone knows what happened there. You can’t keep something like that a secret.”

“But how would his parents have known about it? They aren’t from the area,” CJ said, nodding at Jerry. “Besides, are you sure the realtor would have told them? Maybe he just wanted to sell the house and thought that telling them about the disappearances would have scared them off.”

“Doesn’t the realtor have to tell home buyers about stuff like that?” Jerry asked.

“Maybe so,” Bobby interjected, “On the other hand, after a certain period of time, maybe they don’t.”

“They’re probably supposed to, anyway,” answered CJ. “But my parents used to tell me that even commercials can be misleading.”

“Yeah. Not everyone follows all the rules all the time,” Bobby interrupted. “Maybe the guy who sold your parents that house just *forgot* to tell them about that; figured that after the house was sold, he didn’t care what they found out.”

Jerry thought about it for a minute and decided it didn’t matter under what circumstances his parents had come into possession of the old house. He knew that they didn’t tell him everything, and whether they had this information when the sale was completed or not, he lived there now.

The rest of the school day was fairly uneventful. He met the rest of his teachers. He was given homework assignments and the books he would need to complete them. At the end of the day, he happened to be back in his homeroom for science. Mr. Hong asked for the class to collect their things and prepare for dismissal. Among other things, the end of day announcements included information about the results from the recent elections for the Student Government and the lunch menu for the coming day. Then the voice on the speaker started dismissing grade levels to head out to their respective busses.

When the fifth grade was called to leave, Jerry heaved his now swollen backpack over one shoulder, took his lunchbox in his other hand and stumped to the door. Bobby and CJ met him in the hallway. They exchanged pleasantries as they left the building. CJ turned left down the sidewalk toward the busses at the back of the line, while Bobby and Jerry went to the right.

Once on the bus, Jerry and Bobby sat next to each other toward the back. Jerry was so anxious to get home that he felt almost itchy. Bobby leaned over and whispered in a conspiratorial tone, "You gonna check out that well when you get home."

"Man, I can't wait to get off this bus. I was kind of excited this morning, but now I just can't sit still. It's all I can think about." Even though he was keyed up, Jerry tried to keep his voice low. "You know, I don't know what I expect to find, but I just want to check out that well."

"You want me to come with you? I think Mr. Timberman will let me off at your house." Bobby appeared to be almost as excited as Jerry felt inside.

"Have you ever, you know, checked it out yourself?" inquired Jerry.

Bobby answered, "I've been there a time or two with my dog when we just wander through the woods. Not much to see. The stone well top is still there, but the roof thing is gone and the hole is all boarded up."

"It's boarded up?" Jerry sounded surprised and disappointed at the same time.

"Yeah. Probably keeps other kids from falling in. Nobody wants a law suit, you know."

The bus started to move, pulling across the school parking lot toward the street. Finally Jerry said, "Well, it makes sense, but I just didn't think about that before."

"So, you want some help with your homework... *buddy*?" Bobby's intention had nothing to do with homework, and Jerry understood that.

"Okay. I think it'll be alright with my mom." Jerry said. "I can check with her while they take Becca off the bus."

About 15 minutes later, the boys had secured permission from both Mrs. McAllister and the bus driver. Bobby looked like he had just won the spook house lottery. With his eyes wide and a barely contained grin, he thanked Jerry's mom and the two boys headed into the house, trying not to act too conspicuous. Bobby called his mom to let her know where he was, and agreed to be home by 6:00 for dinner.

In a continued attempt not to draw attention to themselves, they rushed quickly through their homework. Mrs. McAllister brought them each a soda along with a snack tray piled high with cheese, pepperoni, and some crackers. After making sure that they did not need any help with their assignments, she left them again to themselves and pulled the door shut behind her.

"That's all of it," Bobby announced at about 4:40. "I wish school got out earlier."

"I know," Jerry agreed. "Just these last three math problems and I'm done too." Bobby snacked on the pepperoni slices while he repacked his backpack. A few minutes later, Jerry announced the completion of his homework, and closed his book. He didn't bother putting his textbooks away. He just left them in a pile on his desk, and they scrambled down the stairs.

Announcing to his mom that they were going outside, the boys made sure that she would not have a clear view of the well. She was sitting beside Rebecca at the kitchen table with her back to the window, so they slipped out the front door. Certain that they would not be interrupted or questioned about their explorations; they burst out running toward the backyard around the garage end of the house.

The well was not clearly visible from the front yard, or from almost anywhere else, for that matter, but there was only one place it could be. There was a bunch of mature Rhododendrons in the back right corner of the property and they didn't even consider looking anywhere else. The giant shrubs had done well to conceal the old well that hid behind them, and as the boys approached, they were still hard pressed to see any sign of it. As they came upon the curtain of foliage, they started to wander around it, and just as Rebecca had said, it could be seen from deep in the backyard.

As the ruin of an ancient well came fully into view, Jerry froze. He recognized it instantly. He did not know how or when he had seen it before, but he was dead certain that this same well had been burned into his memory cells at some time in his past. He felt drawn to it, as if something was calling him from within. He thought back to the picture of Christopher Pritchard, and the stories about the other boys.

Breaking his pose, he took one step towards the well, then another. Not being aware that he had moved at all, Jerry found himself reaching out to touch the stone ring. In his mind, he began to hear unintelligible voices whispering as quiet as a gentle spring breeze. Unable to make out what they are saying, and bewildered by their very existence, his hand recoiled from the well. As if in a dream, he now saw the well in its original state with the little slate roof and the crank handle, but no rope or bucket. There were no bushes surrounding it now, either. A moderate snow was swirling around him and there was already a light coating on the ground and the well. In the fresh snow, a jumble of footprints had trampled the ground and on the edges of the ring of old stones, it was irregularly compacted and brushed away. The whispery voice began to clear up in his head, and there was an unmistakable panic in the call. "Tom, where are you?" Jerry didn't recognize the name. "Darren, Derrick? ... Come on, guys. This isn't funny." There was also the gentle sound of rushing water, presumably coming from the well. Gripped in anguish, the voice called out again. "Danny? Help me out of here." There was nothing dreamlike about what he saw or heard anymore. He was certain that he was witnessing the events of another time as clearly as if he had been there. And he knew that this was the day that Christopher disappeared. "Mike, go get another rope, wouldcha!!!" Jerry found himself looking across the yard to see five boys walking away. The biggest kid was carrying a football, and they were not looking back or talking to each other.

Turning back to the well, calls from the within were disintegrating to a more tormented wail. Running to the well, he called in, but even as he hollered into the great aperture, his calls were ignored as the kid inside continued to plead with the departing boys. He turned and ran after the other boys, and as he dashed towards them, Jerry was calling to them by name. "Tom! Danny!" Again he met with the same response. Imploring that they return to their companion, he ran in front of them to intercept them, and stood before them screaming in their faces. He couldn't get any response, not even a hint of recognition in their eyes and he realized that these events had come to pass and nothing could ever change them. These were ghosts in Jerry's mind somewhere, and if he stood there any longer, they would pass right through him. The terrified voice started to fade from his awareness, and the snow began to fall heavier until it was so heavy that he was lost in almost total white-out conditions. The Rhododendrons returned and the roof evaporated, but he could still hear his own voice calling, only it sounded like it was miles away. "Chris, wait. Chris... Don't go!"

With that, Jerry found himself fully in his own time rushing to the edge of the sealed well cap with Bobby gaping at him. "Jerry. What are you doing?"

"He needs our help," Jerry snapped back.

"Who do you mean, Chris Pritchard?"

"Bobby, he was calling for help. It was like he was right here." Jerry's breathing was heavy, and his heart was hammering against his ribs. "He was calling for the others."

"Man, this isn't funny. Knock it off." Bobby was starting to get angry.

"No, everything was different. It was snowing and the well was like new and..."

"That's it. I'm outta here," Bobby snarled.

Running after Bobby, Jerry begged him to listen. "No it was real! He was screaming for Derrick and Mike and Tom and the other two; and I saw them walking away with a football over there. When I ran over there; didn't you see them?" Jerry was pointing at the end of the house opposite from the end they used earlier.

Bobby was dazed. He had stopped and was speechlessly staring back at Jerry. After a moment, he finally spoke with a quiet and nervous voice, "Of course not! You never moved. You just stood right there. And instantly you became all weird."

"What do you mean I never moved? I was over there, screaming at those other guys. You must've heard me." Jerry was starting to get frustrated. How come his new friend would not believe him?

"Man, you are really starting to freak me out," Bobby said in a voice that indicated that he was confused. "And how did you know those names?"

"I didn't know them. That's just what the voice from the well was calling out. I promise you, I never heard about any of this before this morning," Jerry replied. "But I have seen this well before. I just don't know when or how."

Bobby looked over at the well.

"He's not there now," Jerry said in a calmer voice. "There was snow and the well was new again."

Bobby looked back to Jerry. "What do mean it was new again?"

"Look, I know it sounds totally crazy, but I didn't just hear the voices, I saw the well right after the Pritchard kid disappeared. It still had that... that roof thingy and the crank handle. There was no bucket or rope and there were no bushes." Jerry was still reeling from the vision. "...And I think the football accident was a hoax. Those other boys; they were walking the other way while Chris was calling for help. You said they might not have liked him too much."

"So they were gonna leave him down there?" Bobby asked.

"That's *exactly* what they did. Don't you get it? They hated him, and had been looking for a way to get back at him."

"Yeah, but..."

"I know it sounds harsh," Jerry replied, "But I think they must have just, you know, had enough."

Bobby still looked like he wasn't sure what to believe. "So what do we do now?"

"We are going to have to get in there, somehow."

The boys stepped apprehensively toward the well together to investigate more closely. The opening of the well was still sealed with several boards that appeared to be nailed in place like the back deck on his house. They had obviously been there for years. They were weathered and gray, and there were slight gaps between them where the boards had dried up and withdrawn from each other. But one of the planks was dislodged, and not quite flush with the others. It looked as if it had been removed, and then not replaced carefully. Jerry reached down to see if it would move. Sure enough, it lifted out with no resistance at all. Looking at the plank he had just removed, Jerry saw that the nail heads were still present on the top of the board, but the pointed end had been shaved or cut from the back. Both boys looked at it, confused. It had obviously been done with the intent of making the board *look* like it was nailed down, yet it was easily removed. The sun was almost down, and when they looked inside, it was as black as midnight. There was a quiet gurgle of water moving below. Thinking back to his vision, Jerry asked Bobby, "Can you always hear water moving in a well? I thought it just stayed still."

"This one's fed by an underground stream that runs out to the quarry. In the papers, they said that when the police were searching for Chris, they dragged the quarry because that's where this thing empties out. From what I understand, this well worked fine until the mining company dug the quarry so deep that it hit this stream," Bobby explained.

Jerry tugged on the next board only to find that it too was free. It had been modified just like the first one, with the illusion of being nailed down, but really just laying there. They pulled up all six boards lying across the top of the hole, and looked in again. With all of the boards out of the way, there was enough light entering the well to see a little farther inside. To their surprise, the top of a ladder extended out of the darkness. Jerry and Bobby looked at each other in disbelief.

Bobby spoke first. “Someone’s already been here.”

“I don’t know,” Jerry said. “It looks like maybe someone has come up from below. I’ve never seen a ladder like that before.”

After a long silence, Jerry finally said, “It’s almost 5:30. You’re gonna have to get home for dinner. Maybe we should see if CJ wants to come over tomorrow evening and we can explore this thing together.”

“We can go in now,” Bobby said.

“I really want to, but by the time we collect flashlights and batteries and anything else we might need, you’ll have to go. I think it would be a really bad idea for me to go it alone,” Jerry said. “Tomorrow is Friday, and we won’t have homework. If I am outside with friends, my mom won’t make me come in until at least 8:00. Do you think you and CJ will be able to come over?”

“I don’t know. I can call him when I get home for dinner,” Bobby responded. They replaced the boards and started for the house. “You don’t really think Chris is still alive, do you?”

“You know, I don’t know what to think,” Jerry answered. “When I had that ... I don’t know ... um ... vision, a few minutes ago, I had the distinct feeling that someone or something was calling me.”

“Maybe you should tell your mom about it,” Bobby suggested.

“Yeah, sure,” Jerry said. Then in a sarcastic voice, “*Hey Mom. How are you. ... Yeah I’m fine. There’s just this one small thing. I had a vision about the well in our backyard and the dead kid who really isn’t dead and he wants me to come and rescue him.* I don’t think she would buy it.”

"Okay. You're right. I'm not even sure I believe it, and I was there." Bobby said. As the boys walked into the house through the front door, Jerry suggested that Bobby write down his phone number so that he could find out what CJ's answer would be. Bobby called his mom and collected his school stuff. Then the two of them waited for Bobby's mother to pull up while they whispered amongst themselves on the front porch.

CHAPTER 5

FINK AND WIZZLE

ON FRIDAY AFTERNOON, all three boys rode home on Jerry's bus. Their backpacks were packed not with schoolbooks, but with work gloves, flashlights and pocketknives. CJ had also brought along a half of a box of a nutty, sweetened cereal and some matches. Bobby had taken about 200 feet of medium weight rope from his dad's workshop along with about a dozen spring-loaded carabineer clips, a folding grappling hook and some other rock climbing hardware. He had even packed a quart-sized plastic bag filled with a trail mix made mostly of peanuts and dried fruits. They were relatively quiet on the bus so as not to arouse suspicions, but once they got to Jerry's house, they ran off the bus, past Aunt Marie's station wagon and into the house before Mrs. McAllister even had Rebecca in her wheelchair.

Amidst all of the excitement, Jerry was still amazed that these other boys had taken such an interest in him. All his life, he had worked so hard to fit in, but CJ and Bobby were sincerely friendly. He was certain that there were no malicious motives driving their friendly overtures. Surely, they would not have been so nice if he had not moved in to such a peculiar circumstance, but they were here nonetheless.

They collected the last of their things into their backpacks. CJ and Bobby each donned a ball cap advertising one of the home teams. Jerry was wearing his favorite rugby shirt and had changed into his weekend jeans. In his pack, he had loaded a can of yellow spray paint as well, his gloves, a Swiss Army Knife and a flashlight. He added in a few packages of cheese crackers, six "D" sized batteries and some water bottles for good measure. Lastly, he went to his dresser, opened up the bottom drawer and pulled out a small black case and tried to put it in his bag discretely.

CJ saw him and inquired, "Whatcha got there?"

"Oh this?" Jerry asked, trying to play it off. "It's just my glasses case."

"I didn't know you wore glasses," CJ said.

"Well, sometimes I have a hard time seeing things far away, and they help in the dark, but it's no big deal. My mom got them for me for school, but I don't like wearing them."

When they got to the first floor, Mrs. McAllister was playing Old Maid at the kitchen table with Rebecca and Aunt Marie. The smell of roast chicken and fresh bread filled the house. Jerry announced that they were going outside.

"Where are you going?" she called after them.

"Just into the woods out back," Jerry answered.

"Dinner's at six-thirty. You will be back of course?" she asked. When Jerry asked if he could have the two boys over after school today, she had offered to feed them all. His normal dinnertime was 5:30, but he asked her to hold it off a little longer so they would have more time outside.

All three boys answered affirmatively that they would be back with plenty of time for dinner. They had every intention of being there. The food smelled wonderful. They opened the front door and scrambled out into the cold.

Each of the boys brought a winter coat and a heavy over-shirt of some kind with them. It was not quite freezing outside, but the temperatures after dark was expected to drop well into the 20's. CJ was wearing his hiking boots, but the other two were in sneakers, and they wore blue jeans.

"So you really had that vision out here?" CJ asked.

"Yeah. It was bizarre. It's like I was right there when it happened, but I couldn't stop it, ya know?" Jerry said. They all understood that he was talking about the day that Christopher Pritchard vanished into the well.

"And you think someone from below has been up here?" CJ sounded nervous. Of the three of them, he was the most cautious. When things looked dangerous in any way, he could usually be found somewhere else. He didn't even really like sledding because you just move too darned fast.

"You sure you don't want me to just hang out here and, you know, let someone know if there's any trouble?" CJ asked. "Because I would do that for you guys."

"Oh give it up," Bobby shot back. "What could go wrong? We have all the necessary safety equipment and Jerry says he is sure that we are supposed to do this. I have never been real big on this extrasensory stuff, but I was here when he had the vision. I'm telling you, I think this is for real." Bobby was talking mostly to convince himself. Inside he was almost too anxious to progress, but he didn't want to be seen as afraid of anything. Bobby reminded CJ that he spent a lot of time online last night reading up on clairvoyant activity, and that Jerry's episode appeared genuine.

Reaching the Rhododendron trees, CJ kept checking back to make sure there was no one watching from the house. He kept his distance while the other two boys removed the decking boards. Bobby took a moment to loop the rope around the base of a young maple tree nearby and test it to make sure that trunk was secure enough. He had already made a loop in the loose end so that they would have it to use as a safety harness in case of a fall. Meanwhile, Jerry peered down into the opening using a high-powered flashlight. The ladder was still there. The flashlight allowed him to see far enough inside to see that it was resting on a pair of planks about two stories deep. It was only about a foot wide and secured to the wall with a few ropes that were tied to some old iron eyehooks embedded in the original mortar. Maybe they weren't ropes. Closer inspection revealed that the ladder seemed to be lashed together with smooth vines. There was water moving below the platform, but it looked as if it was halfway to China. Looking closer at the makeshift bridge, Jerry got the impression that it might almost cross between two tunnels; one on each side.

"Bobby, look at this," Jerry said.

Bobby turned and looked over the edge. "Whoa. That's a long way down."

"Yeah," Jerry countered, "but the ladder looks surprisingly safe. See how green those branches are?"

"It seems to be lashed together pretty well, too." Bobby was admiring the knots that held the rungs on the ladder to the vertical poles. He had been a scout for several years, and had learned a bunch about working with ropes.

Jerry was to be the first one in. He slipped the rope over his head and around his chest. He moved to the well, carefully put one leg over the edge, then the other. The top of the ladder was almost three feet below the rim, so he had to lay on his stomach and dangle his feet in, lowering himself down until his toes connected with the top rung. It felt stable enough. Since the diameter of the well was only about 2½ feet wide, he could reach out to the other side to get his balance if he needed it. Sliding down until his armpits were resting on the edge of the stones, he could reach down to the second rung with his right foot. He was thankful to be wearing work gloves. The rough stones of the well against his cold hands would have been painful and he might have lost his grip. He was wary of each move he made until finally he could grab hold of the top rung with both hands. Climbing down carefully, hand over hand, foot over foot, he made his way down the ladder, mindful not to focus on what lay below. It seemed like a hundred steps to the deck below, but was in reality only about thirty. When he reached it, he called up to the others that he was fine.

"Let the rope go, and I'll send CJ down next." Bobby answered.

When Jerry released his grip on the rope, CJ asked if he could see anything.

"No," Jerry called back up. "There are two tunnels here. One looks like it goes under my yard then splits, and the other goes back into the mountain. The second one goes straight for a long way, but looks like it's just a tunnel."

Bobby finished retrieving the rope and helped CJ into the loop. CJ was so nervous; he almost couldn't convince his legs to go over the wall. He inched himself down to the first rung of the ladder, heaved a great sigh and eased himself down as Jerry had. He relaxed a bit, obviously relieved to have his feet on something solid again. Shining his light back up the shaft, he said, "Boy, it's not gonna be any fun going back up, is it?" He threw off the rope and Bobby hauled it back up. He tied the backpacks onto it, and let them drop slowly to his waiting companions.

When Bobby was ready to come down, he wriggled into the loop. The he wrapped the rope once around the tree and threw the loose end of the rope into the well. The falling rope made a quiet swishing sound, as well as a few gentle smacks as it danced down the walls. Jerry grabbed the loose end of the rope and tugged on the rope to signal Bobby that he had it. With that, Bobby started his descent. No sooner had his foot contacted the top rung than it slipped from the step and he began to fall. The rope snapped tight and slid a couple inches through Jerry's hand. He was so scared that he didn't even notice the burning in his palms. Bobby caught the top edge of the well, knocking his chin hard against the rocks. In an effort to disguise where they had gone, Bobby pulled the boards back across the opening before descending into the well. Ten years ago, six boys left a flurry of footprints in the snow. Today, these three boys left barely a trace in the dead grass. If they ran into trouble, no one would ever know where to look for them.

When all three boys were safe on the subterranean platform, Bobby pulled in the rope while they surveyed their position. The deck was about four feet square, built into a small nook carved from the walls of the well itself. No bigger than most kids' tree forts, the tiny room appeared to have been chipped away by hand. There were neat grooves cut into the top and sides, and crude iron hardware had been driven straight into the rock to which the platform was attached. The rock was very dark gray or even black. The floor was perched like an overlook in a national park high above the rushing torrent below, but there were no railings to keep a careless youngster from falling off. The roughly hewn boards were still fairly green wood. Whoever built the ladder and the platform had done it recently, and expertly. Even the knots that bound everything together looked like they were just tied yesterday. The little vine-ropes were still green and crisp, and did not look at all weathered. The environment was cool and damp, but much warmer than the air above ground.

However, as damp as the air was, the rock walls were surprisingly dry to the touch. In a few places, minute rivulets of water trickled down the sides. A heavy sweater might be all a person would need to stay comfortable.

Training their flashlights below, the gentle flow beneath them looked to be about 50 feet down. The water under them was not truly visible, but the reflections from the flashlights sparkled on the surface and bounced onto the walls near the bottom. A light mist or fog churned quietly at the base of the shaft, indicating that the water might be warmer than the natural air temperature.

The small alcove they stood in was the only place they would be able to stand upright for a while. In both directions, the tunnels' ceilings were slightly lower than the tops of their heads. When they were ready to go on, they would have to duck or crouch a bit. Although Jerry's head was unprotected, CJ wore a Philadelphia Flyers cap and the hat on Bobby's head advertised for the Eagles. Of course, knocking your crown against a ceiling of solid rock was likely to leave a knot with or without a flimsy piece of cotton twill to protect it. The solid stone channels did not appear to be any more natural than the cavity they now occupied. They were very uniform with their almost smooth floor and standardized walls. Mother Nature would not want to take the credit for this work. Her passageways would be beautiful and irregular, carved interestingly with swirling voids and colorful columns. These tubes left one with the impression of mine shafts. The one to the right went into the mountain and was as straight as an Indiana highway. There were no turns or dips as far as their lights would shine. The other went about 30 feet in the direction of Jerry's house and then forked. Maybe forked wasn't the right word. It actually ended abruptly in a "T" shape where it intersected another tunnel. In any case, they had a decision to make.

"So which way do we go?" Bobby inquired of Jerry. As Jerry tried to guess the best route, he noticed that CJ also seemed to be looking to him for the answer.

"What?" Jerry demanded. "You think I know all the answers here?"

"It wasn't our vision." CJ reminded him. "Do you have any ideas?"

"One thing is certain," Bobby said, "It's a good thing that Jerry thought about the spray paint."

Jerry said, "Well, if there was anyone down here, they couldn't have lived in the well shaft for 10 years. People on the news get lost in underground tunnels all the time." Jerry could feel the eyes of his friends on him, pressing him to make a choice. Finally he said, "Before we make any choice, let's see if that tunnel over there shows us anything." He was referring to the tunnel that the shorter one dead-ended into.

The three boys stepped off of the platform onto solid bedrock. The shaft was wide enough for two boys to go through side by side, but they wandered into the underground hallway single file, Jerry first and Bobby at the end. CJ was a bit more uncomfortable than the other two, feeling closed in and gripped by a mild claustrophobia, and preferred not be unprotected from a frontal or rear approach by anything that might emerge from Jerry's visions. Air was flowing almost imperceptibly into their faces and exiting behind them up the well shaft. The walls here had the same look as in the alcove, carved and grooved. But it looked as if the tunneling here was far older than the recently hollowed out niche where they came to rest when they first descended the inverted tower. Reaching the intersection without event, they huddled in the crossroads. This tube went straight like the one behind them, unbending at least as far as the light shone in both directions. It was creepy. There was no way to judge distance, no recognizable features to compare, no horizon. It was almost like riding in the car at night in a heavy fog where you lose track of more than just distance, but even time seems to distort unnaturally. Deep in the left tunnel just beyond the reach of the flashlights, there seemed to Jerry to be movement. It was more something he could feel rather than see. He fished his glasses from his pack and put them on his face, but they did not make it any clearer.

"Do either of you guys see anything down there?" Jerry asked.

Bobby and CJ squinted into the darkness. After a few moments Bobby said, "I don't think so."

CJ disagreed. "I don't know, Jerry. There might be something, but the light just doesn't go far enough ... and I only think I see it when I am looking away."

"So do you think we should go this way?" Bobby asked, looking back at Jerry.

"You guys keep looking to me for the answers. I have never been here either, you know." Jerry was edgy, mostly because this whole thing creeped him out. It occurred to him that he should be thankful that he wasn't claustrophobic.

"Well, I don't know if there is anything moving down there, but there is a draft coming from that direction." Bobby said, pointing to the right. CJ and Jerry looked to the right also and agreed that there was a draft coming from that direction. Again, Bobby implored Jerry to make a choice, not with words, but with a look that did the talking. Meanwhile, CJ was checking out their current space.

To Bobby, Jerry snapped, "It's not like there are signs down here handing out secret messages just for me, you know!"

"I don't know Jerry. There's something scratched into the ceiling here," CJ said. He sounded pretty pleased with himself.

Jerry and Bobby looked up. Sure enough, etched into the stone ceiling was a marker of some kind. All it said was CP, with an arrow under it pointing to the left.

"See," Jerry said, in a light, smart-aleck tone, "Anyone can understand *that* sign!"

"Cool!" CJ exclaimed. "Maybe Chris left that here as a marker to find his way back out."

"Maybe," Bobby said thoughtfully, "But the arrow points the wrong way. The other boys looked confused. "Look," Bobby continued. "If he relied on this marking when he came back this way, it doesn't tell him which tunnel he came from, only which one he went into. If he needed to backtrack several tunnels, he wouldn't know which way he came from at each intersection."

"So do you think it's a trap?" CJ asked.

"I don't think so," Jerry said. The other boys looked at him like they wanted to know what he knew, but Jerry said no more.

"So its this way then?" Bobby said, looking into the left tunnel. He glanced at his watch; 4:25. "I'm not sure we're gonna be back in time for dinner. Hope your mom is not too sticky about that." Bobby was leaning over to pick his pack back up.

"She might get a little upset, but she'll be okay. I think she's just happy that I have some friends to hang out with," Jerry replied.

"You know?" Bobby said, "Caves keep a constant temperature all year round. I think it's about 50 degrees. We might want to trade our winter jackets in for sweatshirts."

"Yeah. It's definitely warmer down here than it was in the back yard," Jerry said. Bobby and CJ opened their bags and retrieved their sweatshirts, putting their jackets back into their packs. Jerry pulled off his jacket and was already wearing the heavy striped rugby, so no trade was needed. The low ceiling did not make it any easier. As he was shoving his jacket into his backpack, Jerry noticed his can of spray paint. He withdrew it and made an arrow on the wall of the tunnel they were leaving behind to show the way back out. They made the turn to the left and started trudging along at as steady a pace as they could muster with their heads hunkered down to avoid the low ceiling. Keeping their flashlights trained in front of them, Jerry and CJ continued to attempt to make out what might be ahead. Bobby kept the rear position, alternately looking ahead and behind.

After what seemed like a half hour, but was probably more like 10 minutes, the boys were already starting to develop fatigue in their legs and lower backs from the crouching. It was at this point that a terrifying thought occurred to Jerry. All of the tunnels were cut to very regular sizes, as if they were used by some kind of train or subway, but there were no tracks. If that were the case, being in one these pipelines could be deadly. He chose to keep this thought to himself. They were too far along their journey now to be able to get to safety before any motorized vehicle could overtake them, and he knew nothing could be gained by adding to everyone's anxiety.

The sense that something was moving just beyond the light was becoming acutely unnerving to all of the three of them. It was however, starting to become more visible. There was a shifting, stirring sensation in the passage ahead of them. Jerry, being in the lead, had the best view of this spectacle. It was not the motion of a creature, but more like the space around them was moving.

"It looks like fog or mist or something. I can't be sure," He said. But that didn't adequately describe it. It was as if the air was alive, yet not alive; like the cave was aware of them!

CJ turned forward. "Yeah, I see it too. It reminds me of those hokey old special effects they used on the original Star Trek series."

Bobby agreed. They walked on together, warily, all looking forward. CJ must have forgotten to be nervous about anyone or anything approaching from the rear. As they came up to the edge of the fog, their flashlights would only penetrate a foot or two. All the while, the mist was churning and shifting, but it was also changing colors. Although there was no real light source of its own, the colors of the cloud faded gently from a soft blue to a warm pink, then to a gentle green. The colors relaxed the boys. Their feelings of anxiety ebbed away while the colors worked their magic.

"I think we are supposed to go into this stuff," Jerry said.

"Normally I would be afraid to do something like that," said CJ, "but this doesn't feel scary. It feels...I don't know, friendly.

"Yeah." Bobby agreed, "But just to be safe, let's hold hands so that we don't become separated." They all agreed that this was a really smart idea.

In single file, with CJ in the middle of course, Jerry reached into the cloud first. The mist did not have any of the qualities of fog that he anticipated. It was not cold or warm. It wasn't moist. As a matter of fact, the only physical sense that was affected by the mysterious vapor was vision. There was, however, some deeper sixth sense aroused by it; a sense that all was well, that it was safe to pass through this strange, alien mass. It seemed to be more of an energy field than a physical phenomenon, yet if it were energy, it was definitely positive energy.

It was immediately apparent that the flashlights would be useless. The light bounced back more than it illuminated. But total darkness was not acceptable either. Jerry backed out and suggested that pointing the lights at the floor might be the best solution as it would ward off the darkness, and would not reflect as badly into their faces. Regardless, they would be walking blindly. Jerry backed out of the mist.

When the three boys were strung together like a family of elephants, Jerry started into the mist again, with his free hand sliding on the wall. The first thing he noticed was that the wall wasn't cold. It generated a gentle warming sensation that seemed to heat up the inside of his hand and forearm. Taking a couple steps into the colored mass, he thought he sensed a rippling motion under his palm and the rock started to feel like it was taking on a more gelatinous consistency. He also began to lose track of time. In what were only a few steps, he was unsure if he had been in the mist for an hour, or a day, or just mere seconds. He could not remember letting go of CJ's hand or the flashlight but he was no longer touching anyone. Light started to filter through the haze, and the wall began to feel more like a slick piece of steel, and it was warm like the stone shaft behind him.

As the mist parted before him, he passed into a lighted room! This was no cave; it looked like a room from a science fiction spaceship. The walls were silver. A long, low table filled the space with kindergarten-sized pedestal chairs almost growing out of the floor. The ceiling was only a few inches above his head, but at least he could stand erect again. The light seemed to be radiating from everywhere and from nowhere at the same time. The one door at the far side of the room was sealed and there were no windows. Awestruck, Jerry tried to take in the significance of his surroundings. At last he remembered... oh yeah! The mist! His friends!

Turning hastily, he saw the colored fog churning in the opening behind him. "CJ! Bobby! Can you hear me?" There was no response. Alarmed, he considered going back in after them. He glanced at his watch. The digital face was blank. Perhaps the battery had died. He was too worried for his friends to give the timepiece another thought. Again he called, and again... nothing.

He had come here to help Christopher, but if he turned back now, he wasn't sure that he would be able to get back. Somehow he felt that the stone passage he had just come from was not on the other side of that cloud. But he could not even consider the idea of continuing without them. Terrified of what might be on the other side of the mist, he saw no other option but to go to the door on the other end of the room and call for help.

There was no door hardware or computer keypads that would open the door, so he pounded on it with his fist. It looked metallic, but gave way to the blows, like it was padded. It was like hitting a thick blanket. This padding absorbed the impact, as well as any sound his fist would have made on a conventional door.

"Hello?" he called. "Is there anyone out there? My friends are missing in the... that misty cloud thing."

Not hearing an immediate answer, Jerry looked back at the swirling fog and saw that the color had changed to a pleasant shade of light purple. He watched for a moment as the movement of the fog appeared to become more uniform, with a distinct pattern that reminded Jerry of a zipper. It started to part and a hand reached out, holding a flashlight!

As Bobby emerged into the room with him, Jerry's heart lifted up. But he entered alone, just as Jerry had. "Where were you?" Jerry blurted out.

"I don't know exactly. In there, I guess," Bobby answered. "Why? How long have you been here?"

"Only a few minutes I think. I can't be sure. Did you let go of CJ?"

"I must have, but I don't remember anything like that." The mist had returned to its random mixing and color shifting.

"Me either. I don't even know how long I was in there," Jerry acknowledged. "You got the time?"

Bobby looked at his watch. "There's nothing here." The face of his digital watch was also blank.

"Odd. My watch batteries quit too." Then he noticed that Bobby's flashlight was also turned off. "When did you turn that off?"

"I don't think I did," he said testing the switch. Off or on, it didn't matter. The flashlight was unresponsive. "That's kinda weird. So, where are we now? And where's CJ?"

"I don't have a clue where we are, but I think CJ's still in there," Jerry answered, nodding at the mist. The boys had been facing each other, but Bobby turned around to look at the doorway of swirling clouds. As he did so, the same phenomena began as the misty doorway phased towards an appealing shade of purple, and unzipped. CJ entered the room, momentarily dazed. With a shudder of confusion, his eyes darted all over the room, and then rested on his friends. "Okay. Now that... that was bizarre!" CJ reported. Then he asked, "Where in the world are we?"

"We don't know. We don't even know *when* we are! Does your watch work?" Jerry asked.

CJ looked at his watch. It was a fancy watch with a digital date and alarm, but the hour and minute hands swept across the face to keep time. Confused, he looked up at his friends. "It says 4:32, but the second hand isn't moving. ... And the digital faces are blank."

Sarcastically, Bobby said, "Oh there's a big surprise."

Jerry opened his mouth to speak when the door on the other end of the room evaporated with a quiet whoosh and two extremely short old men entered. The first one spoke to them as he strode in their direction. "Hello, Jerry." He looked to the other two boys and added, "Bobby. CJ." His voice was higher pitched than Jerry would have expected, and he seemed excited. "I'm Wizzle, and this is my friend Fink. Sorry we're late. Got a bit hung up coming around Lake Nass. Anyway, welcome to Tellusia. Welcome to your new home, boys."

CHAPTER 6

Where in the World...?

"WELCOME TO your new home, boys."

It seemed to hang in the miniature sci-fi conference room. The weight of that statement took the boys' breath away. As the silence found each of them trying to wrap their brains around its meaning, all they found in their heads was more confusion. Their hosts just stood there with anxious grins, waiting for the three boys to absorb the information.

Jerry spoke first. His voice sounded lost and suspicious all at once. "What do you mean our new home?"

Looking excited, the one called Wizzle responded. He was about three feet tall, but the pointed hat added almost another foot to his stature. His hair and beard were pure white. He wore a light green jacket that looked a bit like felt, but was so old looking that it was almost tattered. His dingy ivory shirt had a collar like a t-shirt, but was made from a much coarser fabric. His pants and hat were the same kind of fabric as the jacket, but a darker green. Black boots, which came up to his knees over his pants, were made of some kind of short dense animal fur, and they curled up and around at the toe. And the burnished gold in his belt buckle looked like he never polished it.

"Ah, Yes! That would be the first question, wouldn't it? You will have to remain in this dimension for a while. I am afraid you cannot go back to Pennsylvania through *that* gateway."

"What do you mean this dimension?" Jerry asked.

"Where you come from you are used to calling this planet the Earth, correct?" Wizzle looked at the puzzled boys for some kind of recognition. Their intense stares told him that he was right, so he continued. "In this realm, we have always known of this world as Tellusia. We are currently in the Province of Carrimony in the Kingdom of Sconelund, although we are really about 125 meters below the surface. It is still the same planet that you live on and the same time as well, but this is a different reality from the one you recently departed."

"What are you *talking* about?" Bobby blurted out.

Fink started to answer, but Wizzle cut him off. "Think of it as a different channel on the ...um," He paused. It looked like he was searching for the right word.

Fink helped him out, "Television?" His tone had a bit of satisfaction to it.

"Right, television. Sorry, don't have any of those around here. It would be as if you moved from one program to another. The television is the same, and the program is... ah... broadcasted at the same time, but you are now in a different show!" Wizzle seemed to be having trouble with the names of things that the boys might be familiar with.

"So how come we can't just go back though there?" Bobby asked with a definite tone of irritability as he indicated the swimming mass of mist they had emerged from.

"One way, that one." Fink answered before Wizzle had a chance. Fink was about two inches shorter than Wizzle, but with his taller hat, he stood about the same height. His clothes were similar except that his shirt was black under his coat, and his trousers were a bit better cared for. Fink's hair was more gray than white, and his beard was shorter. The other real difference between the two was the way they carried themselves. Wizzle was friendly and sure enough of himself that he didn't seem to care what others thought of him, while Fink left Jerry with the impression that he was just not to be trusted.

Wizzle shot Fink a cold look and expanded upon his answer. "This gateway is a transdimensional portal, but it only comes. It does not go back. If you tried to reenter your realm though that door, it would spin you around and send you right back here. There are some that go back and forth, and others that only come or go to other times, places or dimensions. But I don't know of any that will take you back where you came from." He looked at Fink who was shaking his head in sad agreement.

"But there might be, I mean a way back, right?" Bobby asked again. To Jerry, Bobby seemed very tense, almost angry with their hosts, but Jerry felt sure that the little men were not responsible for their situation.

Wizzle scrunched his bushy white eyebrows tight with concern. "Perhaps. Shaymalon will know the answer to that better than we," he answered thoughtfully. His voice was still high pitched, but compassionate.

"Shaymalon?" CJ spoke for the first time. "Who is Shaymalon, and as a matter of fact, who are *you*?"

Wizzle took the second question first. "In your reality, we are known to most as Gnomes. Part of our place in the nature of things is to look after all things that are of nature." He grinned, obviously proud of the word play. He continued, "We protect the trees and the creatures and help to maintain the balance between man and his environment... er... Think of us as environmental police. Many of the creatures pushed to extinction in your reality we have simply brought here. In the last several trips to your Earth we have brought back some Caribbean Monk Seals and Tasmanian Tiger-Wolves. There are none in existence in the reality that you have left behind. We did however return a few Ivory-Billed Woodpeckers to a place you know as Arkansas."

"But they've been believed to be extinct since the 1930's," Jerry said excitedly.

"I will tell you this. It is really getting to be quite the undertaking for those of us who live in your realm. Many of the humans, in an effort to survive or from simple greed, are destroying huge tracts of rainforest or wetlands for their own personal gain. We have teams on every continent collecting the endangered species to re-release here."

"And Shaymalon," he continued, "is the Great Prophet. He is the Overseer and our spiritual guide. He told us to meet you here and to escort you to him. He will have the answers you desire."

"You mean you knew we were coming?" Jerry asked.

"Of course we did. Didn't you? You're here to lead us from our bondage and restore peace to Tellusia. It has been foretold across the ages that you would arrive today!" Wizzle said to Jerry in a very serious tone.

"No. I think you have the wrong guy. I'm just a kid; a ten year old boy," Jerry answered.

"There is no mistake. You are Jeremiah Duncan McAllister, right?" Wizzle asked of him.

"Yeah."

"Your friends names are Robert Isaac Schrader and Charles John Powell, right?"

Jerry looked at his new friends. They both nodded.

"You all share the exact same birthday. I believe on your calendar that would be January 15th?"

Now the other two were looking to Jerry for confirmation. As he met their eyes, he got the distinct feeling that his meeting the other two boys was not merely by chance; and he felt that they knew it too. Again, Jerry was confused. These two strangers knew more about him and his new friends than was possible, and they were forecasting him as some kind of savior.

"Okay. Say that I am some sort of hero. What am I supposed to be saving you from?" Jerry inquired dubiously.

Wizzle sighed and looked at Fink. There was an obvious heaviness to the question and neither seemed anxious to answer. Finally, Fink said, "Boys, I think that is a conversation best had with Shaymalon. He's several days journey from here and we should probably get started as soon as possible. The sooner we begin, the sooner we can make camp for today and rest." His shifty air had turned more solemn as he said this, and all the while Wizzle nodded agreement. Jerry sensed a deep sadness from each of the gnomes and decided not to push the subject.

Silence hung in the air for a moment, then Wizzle said, "Well, I guess we had better get st...."

Bobby cut him off in mid sentence, "*Hey!* What about Christopher? We came here because Jerry was sure that Chris needed our help. Is he even alive? Is he here?"

Fink and Wizzle looked at each other quickly then back at the boys. After another serious pause, Wizzle answered slowly. "Yes. He is here. But I am afraid we cannot tell you much. He arrived when he was your age. He was bitter. He had been in the tunnels for hours before he found this gateway. He was hungry and scared and tired. And he does need your help, but as we have said, we will need to let The Overseer provide the details. We are only permitted to give you the information needed to get you to Zaharania, in Neepol, where Shaymalon waits to satisfy *all* of your curiosities."

"But we came because he called to Jerry," CJ pleaded. "Is he okay?"

"We cannot tell you any more than what we have already shared," Wizzle answered him. "It is evening, so we will not travel far today. This cavern runs about 11 kilometers to the main entrance where we should be able to get to the camp before it is too late. Once there, we will share a meal and get some rest for the journey ahead."

"Yeah. Dinner sounds good. So how long will it take us to get to your camp?" CJ asked.

"About two hours." Fink answered with a suppressed grin.

"*Oh man!* I'm starving now!" complained Bobby. "Don't you have anything here?"

"Check your bag," Jerry reminded him.

Remembering the trail mix, Bobby picked up his pack, set it upon the table and opened up the outside pocket. Removing a small plastic bag, he opened it and took out a handful of the snack and tossed some into his mouth. Then he offered some to Jerry and CJ. Jerry declined, but CJ reached into the bag and took a small handful. As he was about to close it back up, he felt the stares of the other two and reluctantly offered some to the gnomes.

Fink shook his head, but Wizzle reached out and asked curiously, "What is it?"

Bobby poured a small amount into the little man's hand and rattled off the ingredient list of different kinds of nuts and dried fruits. He explained how hikers in the wilderness carry it with them to snack on because they use large amounts of energy between meals and humans, being warm blooded, need to keep up their blood sugar. The final ingredient was a tiny candy covered chocolate guaranteed to help with the blood sugar dilemma. The little man nodded approvingly as he chewed on the snack. "Very good indeed," he said.

Jerry was pleased to see that Bobby was trying harder to get along with their guides. He was sure that the coming days would go much smoother if they could all cooperate.

Jerry changed the subject back to their upcoming trek. "So how are we going to travel thousands of miles in only a week?"

"We have some treckers and there is a small gateway station at the southern end of the island by the Great Stone Calendar. It will take us to Bhokatta, Inzia, where we will travel north into the Hummalino Mountains to Neepol. Simple enough, but not without its perils," Wizzle answered as if everyone there was completely familiar with everything he had just said.

The strange new information had been coming so fast that Jerry's head was beginning to hurt. Now he not only had new concepts to deal with, but a whole new collection of words that were very foreign indeed. He had never heard of these places that Wizzle had just rattled off, yet they sounded vaguely familiar to him.

The pause was finally broken when CJ asked, "What is a trecker?"

A brief look of surprise came over the gnomes' faces, and then Fink answered, "We forget how different your technology is from ours. A trecker is one of our forms of transportation here in Sconelund. An Orgachine. Part organism, part machine. It's not really alive, but it's not really a machine either. It's a little bit of both. It recognizes its rider as a friend and will go great lengths for him. It is difficult to explain, but you will understand soon."

"Okay," Bobby said. Acceptance of his situation seemed to be settling over him now.

"Why don't you boys collect your bags, and we will set off," Wizzle said to them.

Bobby reached back over and closed his bag, while the other two picked up theirs from beside their feet and slung them over their shoulders. Bobby hoisted his up on his back as well, and the gnomes turned back toward to the door.

Looking out for the first time, Jerry thought it was dark on the other side, but not as dark as he expected. There was a dim light beyond the doorway that seemed to be moving. It reminded him of what sunlight looked like when it was diffused through the gentle waves of a swimming pool, but it was more yellow. The cave outside the door was still much darker than the room they now occupied. Fink and Wizzle walked toward the open doorway, and the boys followed. As they approached it, Bobby and CJ also noticed the curious lighting in the cave voicing a quiet, shared, "Whoa!"

They filed out one at a time. Wizzle went first, followed by Fink, then the boys. The instant Bobby was beyond the doorway and fully into the cave there was an almost inaudible 'pop' as the door sealed back up again. Turning back to look at it, there was no sign of a door anywhere. The cave simply ended behind them. Jerry now saw the source of the curious lighting sensation in the cavern. Embedded into the walls and ceiling were hundreds of small stones emitting small amounts of light. Most were about the size of a quarter, some were smaller and a few were as large as plums. Each one was surging between being almost off and being as bright as a nightlight. Each of the boys stepped over to the wall like a moth is drawn to a patio light. They had never seen anything like it. Jerry reached out to touch one, wondering if it put off any heat.

"Glowstones," Wizzle replied to the unspoken question. "It's okay. They won't hurt you."

Jerry almost jumped when he touched it. The stone wasn't particularly warm, but he felt a deep warmth radiated throughout his hand and forearm, just like in the mist. But that wasn't all. He had the distinct feeling that he could... sense things.

There were no words for the feeling, except maybe "understanding" or "awareness." He looked at Bobby who had also felt one of the glowstones, but did not appear to have the same mental experience. Nor did CJ on the other side of the passageway. They were looking at their hands, but their eyes were clear and alert. Meeting Wizzle's gaze, he *knew* that the small man understood completely, and he also *knew* that this was a conversation to be had alone out of earshot of the other boys. He guessed there would be time for that later. *Everything* seemed to be a conversation for later with these two. Not looking away from Wizzle, Jerry let his arm fall away from the wall and the feeling of connectedness fell away with it. Then he watched as Bobby and CJ each took their hands down from the wall, and all three of them looked deep into the cave trying to glimpse what lay ahead.

"Shall we?" Wizzle asked. Everyone quietly nodded approval and started slowly marching towards their next stop.

The tunnel was mostly dry, but there were a few slick spots on the floor where some water collected in small puddles. This was a very different passage from the one in Jerry's backyard. The floor and the walls were uneven and very natural looking. There were stalactites above and stalagmites below, and a few columns that almost seemed to be holding the ceiling up.

"Look at that ribbon flowstone," Bobby said in an awed voice. He pointed at a yellowish, translucent 'curtain' hanging down from the ceiling above.

"It looks like it's alive with those stones glowing through it," CJ remarked.

"And do ya see those little tubes? Those are called soda straws. They're probably the beginning of stalactites. Water and um... calcium carbonate I think, drip down and deposit minerals on these tubes. Then one of them blocks up and it grows out and down. It takes like 100 years to grow one inch!" Bobby was so excited about the cave formations; he almost seemed to forget the situation he was in. He turned to Jerry and said, "My dad and I took a trip to a cave in Virginia about a year ago. We learned all about how these things are formed and what causes some of the different colors. Of course, there were none of these flashy stones..."

"Glowstones," Wizzle interjected.

"Right, glowstones. But it was fascinating. That was a much smaller cave, and in one of the rooms, there were a bunch of small bats hanging from the ceiling. Our guide said that they were hibernating. He said that if you touched one, it would probably fall off and die when it hit the floor."

Jerry was thrilled to see the occasional cave spider retreat into a crack in the wall as they walked, but, otherwise, they were alone. Jerry was still wearing his glasses. He usually found they helped a bit in the dark, and although there was some light from the glowstones, it was certainly not daytime here in the underground. At one point, they had to crawl through a gap that was only about three feet tall. It wasn't a real tight space, but it was enough to make anyone feel closed in.

When they entered a room big enough to fit a house into, all three boys gasped at the splendor. The stones scattered in the walls and ceiling gave the impression of supernatural stars twinkling on a clear night in the desert. In all directions, there were pulsating lights. Each one phased on and off at it's own rate, so while it looked like the heavens above, it gave the impression of being much more animated.

"Beautiful, isn't it?" Wizzle said.

CJ answered, "Man. This is incredible." His voice echoed slightly off the walls. "Do you guys come down here often?"

"No," Wizzle answered. "The last time we were here was about ten years ago."

With a start, Jerry turned to face him. "Were you here when Chris arrived?"

"Of course. We have been here for all who have come through that doorway. There have been six others before you; each one about ten years apart. Many of them had different callings than you and Chris, but you all have had special jobs to do," Wizzle answered.

"Really?" Jerry asked.

"Shaymalon has sent two of us to escort each one back to see him. Chris was the last one to come. He was so angry. He wouldn't listen to a word I said to him. I came with another gnome named Stringer that time. Getting Christopher through the cave was a real job. He kept trying to explore the other tunnels and..."

"I haven't seen any other tunnels," Bobby interrupted.

"Oh sure. Well, not yet. As we get nearer to the surface, there are many branches off of the main tunnel. If he had actually separated from us down here, he may not have survived. There have been some who have come exploring here and never returned," Wizzle explained.

"So we finally reached the cave exit. I needed to step into the bushes for a moment and Stringer went to the campsite with Christopher. At that point, the boy attacked him, took all of our food, and vanished into the hills. We never saw him again."

"But I thought you said he was still alive," Jerry said.

"I said he was alive, not that he was with us. We have heard news of him, but it is not always..." Wizzle broke off there. He appeared to be afraid of saying too much, and with that urged the boys to continue.

They walked through the huge underground room, again distracted by the natural beauty of the subterranean landscape, and followed their guides into a narrow passage at the far end. This particular branch of the cave was easily 30 feet tall, but only about a foot and a half wide, even narrower in some places. The boys had to remove their packs and turn sideways to get through these tight gaps in the rock.

After about an hour and a half, Wizzle pointed out the first of what was to be an almost infinite number of branches from the path they were on. Jerry could not imagine what Christopher must have been thinking. Why would anyone want to run off in here when there was someone with you who knew the way out.

"How come there are so many less of those glowstones here?" Bobby asked.

"They only occur abundantly in the deeper parts of the cave. There are a few here, but an additional light source would be helpful," Wizzle answered. With that, he pulled from his pocket a device that looked like a big silver clam with a handle on top. Fink did the same. As they opened up their clamshells, each revealed a large piece of glowstone in one half and a brightly polished and curved mirror in the other. These were much larger than any of the stones the boys had seen to this point and they were brighter too, though they still did not flood all of the shadows with light. And when they pulsed down, the light did not fade out as dark as the smaller ones on the walls.

"Oh man. That is sooo cool." CJ almost drooled over the devices the gnomes had. "Can I see it?" He asked Fink.

"CJ's always been a gadget junkie," Bobby explained.

Fink turned to Wizzle like he was looking for permission, then he held it out to CJ. The boy looked almost hypnotized by the rhythmic pulsating light of the yellow stone. While he looked into the mirror, the light coming from near his chin lent a creepy air to his face as it got darker and brighter. The green brim of his hat didn't detract from that image at all, but gave him an even more demented appearance. He handed the device back to Fink, who looked relieved, and the two little men led the way again.

It had been hard to tell if they were going uphill or down. The floor seemed to be pretty level most of the time until now. Once they entered the area where the caves started branching off in different directions, it became obvious that they were climbing. Jerry's pack was starting to feel heavier and his breathing was becoming more labored.

"How much farther 'til we get outside?" Jerry asked.

"Should only be few more minutes," Fink answered. "But you will most likely want something heavier to wear when we get out there."

"We have our winter jackets with us," CJ answered. "That's why these things are so puffed out," he said, poking at Jerry's backpack.

Moments later, the temperature started dropping, and Jerry noticed a slight breeze. The gnomes started buttoning up their little jackets and turned to the boys.

Wizzle explained, "It's going to be pretty cold. You should put your coats on here. In a minute, we will be outside. The camp is not directly outside the door, as we did not want to alert anyone to our mission. When we exit, Fink and I will conceal the doorway again. As we said, others have gotten lost in here and starved, but that was mostly during a break in. Shortly after Christopher arrived, someone forced his way in. We don't know if it was Chris or not, but if it was, he did not get trapped within the maze of tunnels. He is still very much alive. Otherwise, the cave has always been well hidden. Only after the barrier is blocked will we continue to the campsite."

Having changed into more appropriate outerwear, they proceeded around the next corner. They were met immediately by the sight of the cave's mouth. There were bushy plants obstructing much of the view. Jerry didn't know what else he had been expecting, but he was surprised to see that it was nighttime. They walked out to the end of the tunnel, where Wizzle ducked under the low branches of one of the shrubs. Fink stayed inside and asked the boys for their bags so he could hand them out to his waiting friend. Then Fink motioned the boys out into the night. The air was crisp, though probably not below the freezing point. The almost full moon was well off of the horizon, but was not directly overhead yet, either. The stars out here looked exactly like the ones at home, and the sky was extra clear. A rabbit scurried away, probably due to all the commotion. Wizzle crouched down, walked back through the bushes and held his hand to the wall. He mumbled something that Jerry could not hear, and the mouth of the cave vanished, replaced by what appeared to be solid rock.

"How did he do that?" CJ asked Fink.

"I don't really understand that myself," He replied. "The energy from the glowstone allows us to do many things that would be otherwise impossible. Among other things, the doorways were left here many centuries ago, but with a stone and a true heart, we can control them as needed."

"Wow. That's awesome," CJ said. "Can I try it?"

Fink chuckled a bit. "I don't think so, son. Shaymalon will need to be the one who decides."

Wizzle emerged from the bushes and the five of them set out again, this time across the hilltop with the moon to their left. Luckily, the moonlight was bright enough to light the way. There were no lights in sight anywhere, electric or otherwise. Knee-high weeds were scattered about on the hills. Here and there, taller bushes and rock outcroppings poked out of the ground. Under their feet, the grass was cropped and scrubby. Another rock jutting up out of the ground in front of them was about the same size as the one they had emerged from. It too had several taller bushes growing next to it like the ones by the cave exit.

Cresting the hill, a huge lake came into view below them. It was stunning with the steep hills rising up from it on both sides and the moon reflecting off of it. It looked as if it was lit from within, but Jerry knew that was an illusion.

"That's beautiful," Jerry commented.

"I am always taken by it myself," Wizzle answered. "It's Nass Lake. It is a long..."

"Wait a minute," Jerry interrupted. "Do you mean Loch Ness?"

"Well, yes I suppose I do. We know it as Nass Lake, but you would call it Loch Ness."

"So we are in Scotland?" CJ asked before Wizzle had even finished the answer to Jerry's question.

"Yeah. I guess that's right too," He answered.

"So Inzia, The Hummalino Mountains, are those..." Jerry started.

"India, The Himalayas," CJ finished for him.

"So we are headed for Nepal?" Jerry asked.

They had stopped on the hilltop, and all the while Bobby was staring at the lake. "Is there really a Monster in that lake?" He asked suddenly, without regard to the rest of the conversation.

"No. Well, yes. But not just one, and they're not monsters," Wizzle answered. "There is a family of about six or seven Plesiosaurs still swimming in that water."

"*No Way!* My parents said that was just a myth!" Bobby exclaimed. "I knew it. So how come we can't prove that they live there?"

"Because they live... *here,*" Wizzle said. "Sometimes the portals arise randomly. You might call it a glitch, or an anomaly. Some of the early sightings in your reality of the Loch Ness

Monster were made by people who stepped through a gateway without even realizing it. Then when they ran back to tell friends about it, they ran back through the same gateway, back to their reality and the portal vanished before they could return."

"Whoa," CJ and Bobby mouthed together.

"There are small bands of humans living here too, but here in Sconelund, most of them have come through gateways to find themselves on this side, unable to return," Fink added.

All three boys were staring at the lake, now watching for any sign of movement, but the water was as still as glass, although there was a light steam rising from it at the center.

"It is getting late, and we will need to rest," Wizzle said. "The camp is tucked into that small cluster of trees."

Jerry, CJ and the gnomes started in the direction of the trees that Wizzle indicated, but Bobby had a hard time pulling away. After a moment, he broke his gaze and trotted over to catch up with the others.

Upon reaching the trees, however, the gnomes' moods changed abruptly to solemn panic. Curious about what was the matter, all three boys stepped up to try to get a look. Through some of the branches, Jerry could see that it was a mess. There were shredded blankets and tents. Food items and cooking utensils had been strewn across the ground. Before they could get a better look, the little men turned around and quietly instructed them to move away from the trees. Their campsite had been raided!

CHAPTER 7

Thank Heaven for Little Fairies

THERE WAS A HUSHED panic as the gnomes tried to usher the boys away from the campsite.

"What's going on?" Bobby whispered. The little men were now being cautious and stealthy, as if they thought that whoever had trashed the camp might still be lurking in the vicinity. A finger to his lips, Wizzle guided the boys away from the scene, while Fink circled around to the far side to make sure they were alone.

"I fear that our mission may have been compromised," Wizzle moaned in a very low voice. "If it is true, our journey will be far more perilous. Fink will be back in a moment, and then we can decide on our best course of action."

"But who would want to stop you... or us?" Jerry asked.

"We've told you as much as we can already," Wizzle answered. "Shaymalon gave us our orders, and we are only..."

"Alright!" Bobby said, cutting him off. He had obviously lost his cool again. "That's enough of the secrets. What is going on here? You haven't told us anything about how you knew we were coming or what we're doing here. At least tell us who we're hiding from."

"Oh Bobby, if only I could," Wizzle answered. "There is too much at stake at this moment, and it could put you in too much danger."

"... and what is that terrible smell?" CJ added. Jerry nodded, and Bobby scrunched his nose up a bit as well. Before he could answer, Fink returned from the back of the trees, flanked by what looked like several silver dragonflies darting all over the place and all talking at once.

"Okay. What are those?" Bobby asked.

"I think they may be bush fairies," Wizzle said.

"Did *they* turn the place upside down?" Jerry asked.

"Not likely."

At that point, Fink was close enough to talk in a regular voice. "These are a family of tree fairies. They live nearby. They say they heard the ruckus and came to investigate. When they arrived, Inar's gang was just leaving."

"Who's Inar?" Jerry asked, hoping to get an answer from Fink, who appeared to be too excited to hold his tongue.

"He's the... ohhh... very tricky son. Time will tell, Jerry, but I won't! Not before it's time." Fink answered with a light chuckle.

At the mention of his name, all of the fairies became still and stopped talking at once. The frenzied excitement surrounding the campsite incident was replaced quiet wonderment. After a moment of silence, the youngest looking one flew over closer to Jerry against the urgings from the others to stay put. She was pretty, with long dark brown hair. She wore a silver body suit and white leggings. Two pair of clear wings beat the air behind her as she flew slowly towards him with undeniable curiosity. If she had been human, Jerry would have guessed she was about his age. As she got close enough that Jerry could have reached out and touched her, she hovered in place and looked him over with great interest.

"I believe it's true, mother," She called over her shoulder in a small voice and moved slowly in towards his face. With that, a few of the others flew cautiously nearer. Jerry could feel the air moving from her wings as she almost brushed against his hair. She was so close now that in the bright moonlight he could even see the soft green of her eyes. She had a small nose that only added to her beauty, and an aura of innocence and kindness.

"My name is Clairese." Her voice was small, but clear. "I knew you would come." Some of her family members were nearby now, and they all had the same air of gentleness and purity as Clairese. One of the male fairies flew up beside her and looked right into his eyes. "That's Jacob. He's my younger brother," she said. He might have been younger, but he looked older to Jerry.

"P-Pleased to meet you both," Jerry said, feeling a little awkward about all of the attention.

"The stories of The Ancients have been passed amongst many races here," Wizzle explained. "While most here will rejoice your coming, a few will be terrified that you actually arrived. They will go to any lengths to stop you." He looked at Fink and the other fairies that hung beside him. "Please excuse us." With that, Fink and Wizzle and a couple of the older fairies stepped out of earshot from the boys.

"So will *you* tell us who did this?" Jerry asked Clairese. Just as she was about to answer, her mother flew over and asked the fairy siblings to join them with the gnomes.

"Jerry, I do hope we can talk some more. Good night," she said, and slowly turned away to follow the others over to where Fink and Wizzle were talking with the rest of the tree fairy family.

"Man, what do you suppose they are hiding from us?" Bobby asked of the other two boys.

"I don't know, but it seems to be really important to them to keep it from us," CJ said.

"Yeah. I think something awful has happened here; I mean in this... realm; not just at this campsite," Jerry said. "I just can't imagine why they are hiding it from us. Maybe they think they are protecting us from something, but if there is something we need to be on guard from, I think it would be better if we knew what we were up against."

"Maybe they're the bad guys and they are trying to keep us from learning the truth," said Bobby.

They all looked at the nearby group of gnomes and fairies in conference for a moment.

CJ turned back to Jerry and said, "I doubt it. I'm not sure if I believe everything Fink says, but Wizzle seems genuine."

With that Bobby returned his gaze to his own conversation. "I don't know. We don't know anything about them except that they were waiting for us when we got here. For all we know, this Shaymalon, if that's even his name, is the one that really wants us out of the way. I mean, how do we know that these two aren't trying to keep us away from the *good* guys?"

"I see what you're saying Bobby, but I just don't believe it," Jerry replied.

"I don't know Jerry," CJ said. "He has a point. So far, all we have are their words. There's no evidence that shows what they say is true."

"Oh come off it." Jerry spat, becoming mildly irritated. "Even if they had not shown us the way out of the cave and brought us safely here, who would have torn up everything in their camp?"

"Jerry, that could just be part of the set up!" Bobby implored. "Don't you see, we don't know *anything*."

"... and the fairies? Their reactions couldn't have been staged," Jerry replied.

"Why not?" Bobby shot back.

"Look. I can't explain it. I just know, okay?" Jerry was as sure of this as of how many fingers he had on each hand.

Bobby was starting to get angry. "Like you knew that Christopher needed our help?"

"No... ah, yeah. It's something like that, but not quite the same. I can just *feel* it," Jerry responded.

Of the three boys, CJ was facing the direction of the gnomes. "Something's happening over there," he said. The other boys stopped their bickering and turned to look. Most of the fairies were flying away. Of the ones that were leaving, one stopped at the campsite and suspended above for a moment. The ground behind the trees lit up for a moment then faded back to darkness. It looked like she was doing something there but Jerry could not see anything specific. Fink and Wizzle started back towards the boys, with one fairy following them just over Fink's shoulder. As they approached, Jerry was pretty sure it was Clairese.

"Boy's, here's the deal," Wizzle said in a hushed voice. "Clairese is going to lead us to a safe place to sleep tonight where her family will post a watch. It sounds like it's only a few minutes from here, but they can make sure it's secure. They will also help us to find food before bedding down. Her mother has undone much of the damage to the items in the camp. The treckers have been destroyed and the food has been ruined. Those things cannot be restored. As Fink mentioned, it was a group of Inar's thugs who broke up all of our stuff, but we don't know how he knew we were here."

Bobby opened his mouth like he was about to say something, but Wizzle held his hand up signaling him not to interrupt, then continued. "What we do know is that we won't be safe here. We are going to collect what we need for tonight and follow Clairese.

We will talk when we can be surer that our voices will not be overheard. There are blankets for each of you and we have a large tent. Each of you has your own pack, and that's it. We'll get everything else in the morning. Tonight, we rest." With that, the gnomes turned and walked back to the campsite, and the boys understood that they should follow quietly.

It was a very different scene from what they had witnessed a few, short minutes prior. Everything was neatly bundled, and ready for travel. There was little sign of destruction anywhere. There were however, two long somewhat wide looking bodies lying in oily silver-black puddles on the other side of the clearing. They reminded Jerry of dolphins, although they really looked nothing like a sea mammal. There were 2 sets of what appeared to be enormous dragonfly wings protruding from them, but in the destruction, they were hard to make out. Each one had what looked like three saddles on the top, but they were part of the body, not added on like on a horse. What was probably the front end had what were either ears or antlers or handlebars, he had no idea what they were. The troubling part was several 'wounds' on each one where the oily fluid had run down the sides and onto the ground.

"Those were your vehicles, weren't they? I think you called them treckers," Jerry said, pointing to the dolphin things.

"Yes they were, Jerry," Wizzle said sadly. "Afraid they won't be much good to anyone now. Just hope they didn't suffer much."

"So how did the rest of this stuff get fixed so quickly?" CJ asked.

"Clairese's mother. Look, were gonna have to have this conversation after we set down," Wizzle said, hushing the boys and quietly directing them to gather the things they would need.

With the gear they had been instructed to bring along, the boys followed Clairese and the gnomes into a shallow cave about ten minutes away. It was more of an overhang really, but offered some additional shelter against any gusts that might blow up overnight.

Bobby reluctantly offered to help them set up the tent and set out the blankets. His outdoorsy background really came in handy. Once the sleeping arrangements were attended to, food needed to be the next item addressed and the two gnomes opened up a folding table. It was not as tall as they were used to, but it would do the job. They set out silverware and some small metal plates and cups. He didn't know what time it really was as his watch no longer worked, but Jerry guessed that he was probably about four hours late for dinner at home, making it around 10:30.

"So, you said the fairies were taking care of food for us?" CJ asked Wizzle. Typically shy, he must have been hungry to come up with that question.

"It should be along in a few moments," He assured the boy. With that, Clairese's mother and another older female fairy flew in empty-handed. The boys looked on in disbelief. How were they going to make it through the night? They were ravenously hungry and sleep would surely not come easy.

"Dinner is served," The older fairy said and with that she spread her arms. A glow appeared upon the table that left a small feast behind as it dissipated.

"Whoa," The boys all said together. They had seen a lot of amazing things today, but this topped everything so far.

Jerry looked at Wizzle and asked, "How did she do that. Don't you need a wand for magic like that?"

Wizzle laughed a full belly laugh. "Don't be daft, boy. You can't get magic from a stick. Where did you ever hear such rubbish?"

"I don't know really. It just seems to be what I've always thought. That's probably just how they are shown on TV and in the movies." Jerry saw a confused look on Wizzle's face and clarified his last statement. "Television."

"Well that may be the way they are portrayed in your fantasy entertainment programs, but this is how fairies really work their magic. It comes from inside, like a thought they can project out," Wizzle explained, still chuckling a bit.

Dinner included a hearty stew with big hunks of meat, carrots, onions and potatoes. There was some kind of heavy bread with raisins and grains baked into it. The only drink was water, but it might as well have been a liqueur from the heavens. They were all so hungry, so thirsty, that even bad food would have tasted good, and this was not bad food. It was delightful. Everyone ate as much as they wanted, and there always seemed to be more. Jerry ate everything, even the meat chunks in the stew, but thought it odd that the gnomes, self proclaimed environmental police, ate the meat with great delight. Dinner was followed by a cake that none of the boys had seen or tasted before. Chocolaty and fruity at the same time, it was heavenly.

Even through all the merriment, there was still an undeniable tension. The fairies had brought the food, but did not sit down with them to enjoy any of it. Perhaps they had eaten already. They were positioned all around the camp in the treetops and above the tent watching for signs of intruders. Only Clairese stayed nearby, flitting around above the table, occasionally landing on the end for a rest, but to Jerry, even she seemed nervous.

After dinner, the post dinner mess was whisked away by the older woman fairy, and Fink, Wizzle and the boys slipped into the tent. It was toasty warm inside, but there was no fire. Light was coming from the gnomes' glowstones, but they were pulsating in unison rather than individually.

"How can it be so warm in here?" Bobby asked.

"The Glowstones," Fink answered.

"But they weren't warm when we touched them in the cave," CJ said.

"One, no. Two or more will produce great warmth when placed together," Fink continued. "They sync with each other to release great amounts of energy."

"Is that why they are blinking together?" Jerry asked. CJ had wandered over to the center of the tent and reached down to feel the heat from them, but it was no warmer immediately beside them than it was as they wandered into the tent.

"Theirs is the power of Mukanah. It is the great energy that runs through all of nature," Wizzle explained. "It is the force that keeps harmony and peace, without which the universe would simply cease to exist. When brought together, these mere stones can do the unimaginable."

Jerry thought he might be dreaming. Everything he had seen since he climbed down the well shaft left him amazed. It was all so wondrous, although some was a bit scary. But, if he were dreaming, would it all be in color? Would he smell the aromas of the food and feel the cold air and the cool walls of the cave. The events he was witnessing were fantastic, but there was no dreamlike quality to the experience of it. No, the thought that he might be asleep was plausible, but this was too real to be a dream.

"You said that when we had a quiet time and place to talk, you would tell us who Inar is." Bobby had changed the subject.

"No. I said we would talk," Wizzle answered.

"Inar's an evil dude, isn't he?" Jerry asked.

"Jerry, look. We can only tell you this, and I believe Shaymalon would approve under the circumstances. As Bobby said, we should at least show the courtesy of letting you know who we are trying to protect you from," Wizzle answered, glancing at Fink. "Inar the Iron Fisted. He's a Sasquatch. You may know him as Bigfoot. His family has terrorized Tellusia for thousands of years. When the North American Indian tribes learned to plant and harvest vegetables and fruits, some of the Sasquatch would steal the crops right before they were ready to pick. Of course the farmers got mad and set traps or hunted and killed the thieves. Well, most of the Sasquatch ran, but a few became bitter and vengeful, vowing to destroy mankind. Nonetheless, they were still hunted and kept at bay by the humans in your dimension. Then one day, one of Inar's ancestors slipped through a portal from Earth to Tellusia. This one was a two way gateway, and they could go back and forth."

"So that's why they are seen on Earth, but only occasionally?" Jerry asked.

"Yes," Wizzle answered.

Fink added, "If one of them should die in your dimension, others retrieve the body, thus leaving no credible evidence of their existence on Earth. The ones who claim to have seen a Sasquatch are shunned and ridiculed, so the Bigfoots can come and go between dimensions without fearing any real organized resistance."

The wheels in Bobby's head had obviously been turning too. "So all we have to do is get to the portal they use and we can go back home?"

"It's not that simple, Bobby," Wizzle answered. "Inar's gang controls that portal. Won't let anyone near it. Trying to get back to your home through there would be suicide."

"So are all of the portals controlled by Bigfoots?" Jerry asked.

"I can say only this much more. They do not control any other gateways, but they will probably dog our footsteps clear to Neepol," Wizzle answered. "But we must stop talking and get some rest. Tomorrow will be a very long day."

"Hope you boys don't mind walking a bit," Fink added, a devious grin on his face.

With that, everyone started to get comfortable for the night.

"I have one more question," CJ said. "Did you guys make the ladder that we used to climb down the well shaft?"

"No," Wizzle answered. "A couple of our boys on your side of the gateway put that together for you. Why do you ask?"

"Well, you said that you could not get us home through that portal, right?"

"Right."

"It just bothered me a little. If you had been the ones who had built the ladder, I would have been really curious as to how you got there and back, yet we wouldn't be able to," CJ answered back. "But it seems that we may really be stuck here for now."

"I wish for you that it weren't so," Wizzle replied. "Home is a place you should always be allowed to go back to."

"I already miss my parents. I hope I get to see them again," CJ added, to no one in particular.

"So do I, son," Wizzle answered quietly.

The tent was not dark, but it was warm. There was not so much as a breeze outside, but the air would have been too cold to sleep comfortably. Before slipping under his blanket, Jerry took off his glasses and slid them into their case and tucked it into the outside pocket of his pack. In spite of the predicament he was in, he sent up a silent, but heartfelt prayer, thanking God for his protection and the camaraderie. The pulsating light lulled him towards sleep as gently as the waves lapping at the shore of a lake on a still, summer night.

In the quiet, Jerry looked back over the last few days. He had had the premonition about Aunt Marie's car accident. None of his earlier deja vu episodes had ever been quite so vivid. The new house really wasn't so bad. It was just a house. He had met Bobby, and then CJ. He learned about the legend of Christopher Pritchard. Then he learned that it was no legend. He wondered about what had happened to Chris, and to the other boys as well.

He considered all the new people in his life. Bobby was outgoing and charismatic, a true sportsman. CJ was a bit more cautious. He was shy, but extremely logical and very intelligent. Jerry envied CJ's innate ability to understand and use computers and other gadgets. Wizzle was a competent leader as the captain of a small band of travelers and kept his head in a pinch, though he would probably not do as well trying to lead a nation. He could not get a good read on Fink yet. He seemed helpful, but there was still something untrustworthy about him. And he thought of Clairese and her family. Had it not been for their compassion, Jerry wondered if he would even be alive right now. If so, he certainly would have been hungrier.

Then Jerry thought about what he had to offer in this little venture. He was adventurous, if not a bit careless. The thrill of bike jumping had landed him in the emergency room on more than one occasion. But bike stunts also carried with it the necessity to learn how to maintain his own bicycle. He had even been told once by his father that he was a better bike mechanic than his father ever had been. And dropping down an unknown well without telling any adults where he was going now seemed a bit foolhardy. His knowledge of comic books was probably not going to get them out of any real fixes. That was not how the real world worked, *but was this the real world?* And did his visions and premonitions help him or hurt him? There was no way to know now. One premonition had saved him from a potentially deadly car accident, while the vision of Chris Pritchard may have gotten him into more trouble than he knew how to get out of.

He remembered with some clarity two years ago seeing his sister laying at the foot of the stairs in a heap, and *then* hearing her scream as she tumbled to the ground floor. That was the first time he ever experienced one of those crazy visions in his head. He'd had a few others since then, but except for the most recent ones, none of the others really stuck with him. This sixth sense could be a blessing or a curse. Time would be the only way to know which it would be. And when he touched the glowstones, he had the sensation of being connected to the whole universe. He alone had that experience. It was clear that the other two boys had not. And now he had been told that he was expected to save the world; even if it was not *his* world. He could not imagine how his little shoulders would be strong enough to carry a burden that at one time had been left to the mighty Atlas, according to Greek Mythology.

Turning his thoughts to the coming day, Jerry contemplated what new wonders and dangers lie ahead. But these thoughts never got the chance to take shape. Through sheer exhaustion and the droning yellow light, sleep came swiftly.

CHAPTER 8

Merry-Go-Round Animals

"GOOD MORNING BOYS. Beautiful day! Time get up and move on," Wizzle announced in an excited voice. It took Jerry a minute to realize that the dream he remembered having was no dream. It was real. The little men and the tent were still there, even now that he was no longer asleep. Fink was presumably outside tending to breakfast. The smell of bacon, eggs and coffee and maybe some kind of bread all mingled together and drifted in on the morning air.

The boys all slowly pushed off their blankets, put their clothes back on before they stepped outside. Forgetting that it was still November outside, the chilly air was a shock. Jerry turned from the door of the tent, retrieved his shoes and jacket and went outside. The other two boys did likewise and they sat around the low table to share breakfast.

"We have scrambled eggs, bacon, wheat toast, butter and goat's milk. Take what you like and pass it on," Fink said to the boys.

"These eggs are delicious, Fink," CJ said to him.

"Thanks," He answered. "Ostrich eggs. Only needed one of 'em to feed the whole lot of ya," he said with a slight snicker, not masking the satisfaction that swelled in him from the compliment.

"I thought they came from Africa!" Jerry snapped.

"You know your animals, boy," Fink answered him. "In your realm, they used to live far beyond where you call Africa. They used roam through much of Azzia and Urappe. Here they still do!"

"So how did you cook this stuff?" Bobby asked him.

"Remember those Glowstones that heated the tent last night?" Fink asked him.

"Sure."

"They can really heat up. Don't put off any smoke, either. Good thing, too. Smoke might give our position away."

"But they weren't that hot when I reached out to them last night in the tent. Just warm," CJ said in an inquiring voice.

"You gotta know how to *talk* to 'em," Fink answered.

CJ looked confused. "You mean like the magic words?"

"More like magic *thoughts,*" Wizzle answered from the other end of the table. "The stones respond best to those who are pure of heart. The user forms a bond of sorts with the stone. They have a natural state of warmth, external warmth without being warm to the touch. It's a function of Mukanah. The energy comes from within all life, but is radiated out through the stone."

CJ looked lost in amazement, but Bobby had something else on his mind. "So, what's the plan today?"

"We begin," Wizzle answered. "We have about 750 kilometers to go before we leave the island."

"Whoa. This is a big island," Bobby replied. "How long is that gonna take?"

"On foot, without any complications, it would take a little more than two weeks," Wizzle answered. "But the McKleskys have arranged for transportation for each of us."

"Who are the McKleskys?" CJ asked.

"They're the fairies," Wizzle answered. "The whole family will be stopping by in a little while with some ostriches to replace the ruined treckers."

"We're going to ride on ostriches?" Bobby asked.

"Sure. They're strong and fast. We should be able to stay out of Inar's reach on 'em," Said Wizzle. "Why, they can run up to about 65 kilometers per hour."

"But that's their top speed," Jerry added. "You can't ride them at that speed for long, but I would bet you can ride them at half that speed for a longer distance."

"That's probably about right," Wizzle replied.

"That's still about 24 hours riding time," CJ calculated.

"True. But three days travel time is a whole lot better than 16 or 17," Wizzle noted.

Bobby was laughing. "The last time I rode an ostrich, it was on a merry-go-round. And it didn't move at any 65 miles per hour; that's for sure."

"Not 65 *miles* per hour; 65 kilometers per hour," CJ answered him seriously.

"What's the difference?" Bobby asked, still giggling.

"65 kilometers per hour would be somewhere around 40 miles per hour. We're estimating that an ostrich can run at a *sustained* speed of about 18 to 19 miles per hour. On a bike, you're lucky to average over 10," CJ always did take his math seriously, and Bobby got over his giggles.

"But what is this merry-go-round?" Wizzle asked.

"It's a ride at the amusement park. It's just for fun, but it doesn't actually take you anywhere. It just goes around and around and around," Jerry answered him.

"But why doesn't the bird get bored and run away?"

"They use plastic or wooden models of animals on the ride. A lot of people really like riding them," Jerry answered back, a slight smile tugging at the edges of his small mouth.

The five companions finished eating, cleaned up and started packing up the campsite. Just as Wizzle and Bobby got the tent securely packed, the fairies appeared over the edge of the small hill that blocked their view of the surrounding landscape. They were followed by seven ostriches. The thing that really struck Jerry as odd about the whole scene was that the animals related better to the fairies than circus animals responded to their trainers. Five of them stayed beyond the edge of the campsite, while the other two walked straight into the center of everything, folded their legs and lowered their broad bodies to rest on the ground. One of them already had a pack on his back. Apparently, one of the fairies gathered up the remainder of their gear from the original campsite by the cave so they would not have to go back there.

"Thank you Marisha, John," Wizzle said to the elder fairies.

"We are honored to assist you in this endeavor. These boys *must* be delivered safely," said the one that Wizzle called Marisha.

"If you need anything else, please send Jacob and we will come as quickly as we can," Mr. McKlesky added.

"So Jacob will be coming with us?" Jerry asked Fink.

"Yes. And Clairese, too," said Fink.

"Bobby. CJ. Gimme a hand with this stuff, will ya?" Wizzle asked. The boys stepped over to him, and started lifting packs and tents onto the two birds beside the piles of camping gear. They got everything on their backs, and Bobby helped tie the last of the knots to hold it all in place.

Next they rigged some crude, but effective, reins onto the other five ostriches using some of Bobby's rope. That would make them at least a little easier to ride. "So how come they let us do this to them?" Jerry asked Fink.

"The fairies have a very special relationship with the local creatures. Look out for them, they do. So the animals don't mind helping them out from time to time," Fink said.

"So can they talk to the animals?" Jerry thought of the old Dr. Dolittle story as he asked the question.

"You might say that. It's a bit more like telepathy, I think. No language barriers, you know?" Fink seemed different this morning. He was more comfortable maybe, not so nervous. Whatever it was, Jerry's distrust of him was starting to drop away.

A few minutes later, they were ready to go. The ostriches all squatted down so that they could be mounted. Everyone climbed onto one of the giant birds and they stood back up. Jerry had a ticklish feeling in his stomach as the bird rose quickly, bobbed a bit from front to back and found its balance. CJ let out a short laugh as *his* animal stood up.

They all tried to urge their birds forward to see if they would be able to control the animals. Clairese hovered in next to Jerry's ear and whispered, "*Think* what you want him to do. He will listen,"

Meanwhile, Wizzle and Fink were working with Bobby and CJ, explaining the basics of handling the great birds. He heard Bobby mention that it was just like a horse and CJ seemed to be getting the hang of it too.

Jerry tried concentrating on turning left. The ostrich turned his head to the left, but did not move. He considered going forward, and the bird took a step or two, and stopped.

"You're trying too hard. Your thoughts are becoming clouded by your desire for them to be heard. Relax, and he will hear you better," Clairese said.

He looked over his shoulder at the bushes on the far side of the camp. He thought to himself that he might want to try to get the bird to take him there. No sooner had the thought emerged than the ostrich turned around and walked slowly to where he had just been looking. The bird bobbed up and down, and with each step he lurched forward. This was going to work okay, but finding his balance was going to take some practice. CJ and Bobby seemed to be achieving a bit of success with their rides as well.

"Woo-hoo! This is *nothing* like a merry-go-round ride," Bobby assured them all.

When everyone seemed comfortable enough on their mounts, Wizzle signaled to them to move up and out of the trough that had been their campsite the previous night. Clairese and Jacob followed, while the rest of the McKlesky family stayed behind, waving goodbye. As they cleared the rise, the site of the countryside and the lake extracted gasps of amazement from each of the boys. Dark green fields rolled out to the horizon to the right. The land in this direction was broken only by an occasional rock wall or small stone house with a thatched roof. Thin trails of smoke rose from the chimneys. Jerry could only assume that the occupants of these homes did not use the glowstones to heat them. He imagined that if God were to make a patchwork quilt, it would look like this. A gravel or dirt road snaked through here as far as could be seen. On the left, some mountains rose from the ground like a great wall in the distance, barring any potential invaders. They weren't huge mountains in geologic terms, but foreboding nonetheless. Shadows of the sparse puffy clouds crawled down the slopes towards them.

Directly before them lay the lake, Nass Lake. It filled the valley between them and the mountains on the far side like a bright blue mirror. In the water, Jerry half expected to see a plesiosaur gliding through the water, but nothing stirred the surface. The reflection on the lake showed the upside down image of the mountain on the other side with the sky and moving clouds in the foreground. He had the impression that he was looking at two worlds at the same time, and that he might be able to walk through that reflection into his own realm and return home. He suspected, however, that even in this reality that you could not walk through mirrors or even reach the end of a rainbow.

"We should probably be going. The sun will be working its way towards the top of the sky, and before you know it we will need to set up camp again," Wizzle stated. He pointed towards the gravel road and told them that it was the way they had to go. Out of habit, Jerry glanced at his watch. It was of course still blank, but he guessed it was around 9:00 in the morning. The boys bobbed awkwardly, pushing their ostriches in the direction of the road. It was not the smoothest ride, but it was faster than walking.

He thought of Kyle back in Minnesota and wished he could see this. He was hanging with gnomes and fairies. He was riding an ostrich. He was beside the famous Loch Ness, and even had a reasonable chance of spotting its elusive monster. And, perhaps most importantly, he had made friends with a couple of regular guys. *Regular guys!* Hopefully he would have a chance one day to tell his old friend, he thought. Then he realized that if he ever got the chance to tell anyone about this, there was no way they would believe him. No, even if he ever did get home, he would probably have to keep this whole adventure a secret for the rest of his days. Well... maybe not the part about the two new friends from school. That part was extraordinary, but normal.

The boys were still in awe of the scenery. Where the bases of the hills met in minute valleys, rows of trees marked the low points. There were pastures with sheep and goats scattered amongst them. The black surfaces of the ponds and lakes were trapped between the hills like tidal pools on a rocky beach. As the morning wore on, the boys found that they no longer needed their winter jackets and they secured them onto the pack animals.

The conversation mostly centered on the landscape for a while, but eventually turned to questions that had left them wanting for answers yesterday.

"So how come our watches and flashlights don't work?" Jerry asked.

Both of the gnomes seemed to be thinking about that and finally Fink said, "I guess that the energy source for your instruments isn't compatible with Mukanah."

"So there is no kind of electricity here?" CJ asked.

"I don't think so," Fink answered.

"How about storms? Do you ever have thunder storms?" CJ asked, still trying to get an explanation that made sense.

"Well, sure. Sometimes."

"During a thunder storm, that flash of light is electricity traveling from one place to another."

"Is it the same electricity that powers your flashlights?"

"It's pretty much the same," CJ answered.

"I think Fink is right," Wizzle put in. "We do have those thunder storms, but the lightning never strikes anywhere near the glowstones. It probably can't exist in the same area as any kind of Mukanah link."

Ahead of them, the road forked in two directions. The path to the right went down hill while the tracks to the left went up. There was a tree just down the path to the right that looked like a giant letter "Y". There were no leaves, and its brown dead trunk looked like it could fall at any minute. Something about the tree brought a chill to Jerry. As they neared the fork, Wizzle indicated that they would be taking the low trail to the right. Jerry suddenly became apprehensive and he found his hands were shaking. Unaware of his having done so, he reached to touch his forehead, and found that his brow was sweating. His sight began to cloud up, as if tears were filling his eyes. The scenery before him faded from view and the now familiar cloud started to swim around in his eyes and snake into his brain.

As the fog started to clear, he could see a gravel path and a rock wall. The wall wasn't tall, maybe 2 ½ feet. It was built of all sizes of rocks piled on top of each other without the aid of cement or mortar. Flies were everywhere, buzzing in drunken circles. Lying just beside the path was a sneaker. It was a Nike court shoe, just like the ones Jerry himself wore. It looked *exactly* like his own shoe, right down to the rip in the heel. No. It *was* his shoe. Why was his shoe on the roadside, Jerry wondered? Was this another possible future? He knew it was. It was paused for his convenience, so he could study every detail, just like the car wreck that never happened.

Not far from the abandoned sneaker, an ostrich lay. His neck was bent unnaturally, leaving no question that it was dead. Another shoe, this one black. And a pointed hat; Wizzle's pointed hat. And there was blood on it. Again, Jerry had the sensation of walking through the scene as a person might walk through a dream. Nothing interrupted or disturbed his concentration as he walked through the destruction. He was free to explore every detail.

The next thing his attention was drawn to was the baseball cap. Black, with a green and white eagle's head proudly stitched across the front of it, Jerry knew this hat. He didn't want to see what he knew was coming next. The hat was lying on the ground beside a child. A boy his age, with black hair and a brown sweatshirt. The kid's face was obscured, mostly because it was face-down on the road, but partly because the shadows fell across it in a way that just distorted the visible features into something unrecognizable and hideous. There was blood on his shirt and the stones under his head were soaked with it as well. Knowing it was Bobby; Jerry wanted to turn away but could not.

When he was finally ready to look at the next detail in the big picture, it came not to his eyes, but to his nose. An awful stench hung in the air. It had several components. One part of it smelled like wet dog and old gym socks stirred together in a dirty garbage container, just like the stench at the ruined campsite last night. Another element was blood with its almost metallic, organic aroma. But the worst was the faint, but unmistakable odor of death. Not the scent of rot or decay; this was more like an unconscious awareness of lives recently snuffed out by some malignant presence. The flies, the deformed bodies, the baseball hat, Jerry's sneaker... and the blood. The red-black splashes and smears of the blood in the dirt and on the rocks. Jerry was beginning to feel nauseous and was ready to leave. Searching for the way back to reality, he turned around to look behind himself. The old, dead, "Y" shaped tree was back there, acting as a beacon or a marker buoy on the harbor. It pointed the way from where he was now in his mind and spirit, to where he had left his body behind. The vision had shown him that they were about to be attacked on the road to the right!

"Wizzle, we can't go that way!" Jerry cried as he snapped back to present time. He was somehow surprised by the sense of urgency in his own voice.

CHAPTER 9

Crawford's Glenn

"BUT IT IS the short way," Wizzle answered.

"We have to go the other way. How much longer is it?"

"It'll add a few hours to our travels," Wizzle answered.

"But it will get us where we need to go, right?"

"Eventually. Why?"

"There is going to be an ambush down there," Jerry answered pointing down the road on the right. With that, Wizzle looked at Jacob and Clairese who immediately sped off in the direction Jerry had indicated, being careful to stay out of sight and out of reach. As they vanished from view, Bobby and CJ each threw Jerry a concerned glance before turning back to watch the fairies shrink and disappear into the distance. The five of them sat and waited anxiously for their scouts to return. Even the ostriches seemed to be nervous. Jerry could see the rock wall from his premonition in the distance, maybe a mile away. No one was visible on the other side of it, but he knew they were there. It occurred to Jerry that they were standing out in the open, where anyone or anything could see them clearly even at this distance.

He whispered to Wizzle, "I think we had better move out of sight."

No one said a word. Wizzle gestured for everyone to follow him, and they moved over towards the high road, behind the hill and out of view from the distant wall. Wizzle slid off his bird and handed his hat to Fink. With that, he slowly moved out to a point where he could see down the road. If they were about to be attacked, everyone knew they would need as much warning as possible to get a head start on their enemy. The minutes dragged on, feeling like hours.

Finally, coming from behind them down the high road, Clairese and Jacob reappeared without much warning. Jacob said, "He's right. Inar's men. Seven of them, with clubs, axes, nets and incinerators."

"Were you seen?" Wizzle asked.

"I don't think so," Clairese answered. "They were mostly trying to stay concealed. That takes some effort. They are too big to easily hide in such a small space. One of them kept glancing this way, but you must have been too far away to be seen."

"Transportation?" Wizzle asked.

"I didn't see anything," Jacob answered nervously. "But it might be somewhere else out of sight."

He flew around the edge of the hill to make sure that the would-be attackers were still in their position. With a gasp, he whizzed back. "They're coming!" He shouted, though his voice was so small that it did not really sound like a yell.

"But how did they know?" Jerry asked.

"They must've seen us before we ducked in behind the hill," Wizzle answered.

While Wizzle was returning to his ostrich, Fink darted out into the open for a second to survey their options.

"They're at a full run, but on foot. And they've covered about a third of the distance while we have just stood here. Come on."

And with that, Fink steered his ride up the hill. The rest of them scrambled up the road behind him.

"They can move fairly fast, but I think the birds will prove faster," Wizzle called from behind. The ones with the camping gear were right on his tail. "Clairese, Jacob. Anything you can do to slow 'em down?"

Thinking for a moment, the fairies turned back in the direction of the assailants. They looked like they were headed back to the forked tree. Sure enough, the tree lifted out of the ground, roots and all. It levitated there for a brief second, then it turned sideways and vanished behind the hill. They could all hear the grunting and shouting as the giants thundered toward them. There was a collective holler of pain and surprise as the tree must have struck them. Jerry imagined they were lying in a heap, but he could tell from the sounds over the edge of the hill that they were still on the move. Again the collection of Bigfoot was heard to cry out and groan. It sounded like a football game on a Sunday afternoon, and the play had just begun.

With the wind in his hair as he was whisked up the hill at a dizzying speed, the sounds of the beasts pursuing them were getting more difficult to hear. Climbing higher up the slope, the road moved closer to a cliff so that to his right, Jerry could see the scene below. Clairese and Jacob had indeed been bowling for Sasquatch, and it looked like the last ball rolled a strike. Seven big brown hairy ape-men were splayed out on the ground with a tree across their backs. They had been struck from the rear as they retreated. Awkwardly throwing it off, one of them pulled a weapon from his side and aimed it into the air. From this distance, he could not see the fairies, but he assumed that they were the target. A flame shot from the weapon, arced into the air above him and vanished. The others all made it to their feet and echoed the first Sasquatch, hoisting crude flamethrowers onto their shoulders and spitting fire into the air.

Terrified that the fairies might have been hit, Jerry wanted to turn around to help the small siblings. He intuitively knew that this would be suicide, and continued riding with the rest of his companions. When the tree lay there motionless for several moments, he was sure that his fears had been confirmed. Wouldn't they heave the giant stick at their adversaries again if they were able? The enemy just stood there for an instant, put away their weapons and started running again. They were surprisingly fast for bipeds, but nowhere near as fast as the ostrich gang. There was still no sign of Clairese or Jacob. The big birds had their necks stretched out in front of them, running as fast as their long legs would carry them. Higher. Higher. As they neared the top of the hill, the path narrowed to only a few feet wide. The cliff on the right was joined by a cliff on the left. To the right, the group of Sasquatch was small in the distance. The thought passed through Jerry's head that they looked like ants from up here, but it was a cliché, and it wasn't accurate. They were shrinking below him, but they did not even resemble ants. They were not far enough away yet for the creatures to look like anything other than hairy men. On his left side, the hillside had given way to a cliff that dropped off almost straight to the lake below. It was even farther below him than the ground on the right. It didn't matter, though. Dropping off of either side would mean certain death. He thought to himself, *Don't look down. Don't look down*. Onward they raced as fast as the animals could move.

A large bug seemed to be stalking Jerry now and he swatted at it without looking.

"Hey!" Clairese yelled in his ear.

"Ohmigosh! I'm sorry. Are you okay? Where's Jacob," Jerry inquired.

"Yeah, fine. Jacob is back talking to Wizzle."

Jerry glanced over his shoulder. "You were magnificent. You just move those things with your mind?"

"Sure. I never even think about it. You can too, you know?" she replied.

He was not sure what she meant and was about to ask when Wizzle called from the rear to slow down. "We are going to wear these creatures out if we continue at this pace."

"I really don't like it here," CJ said to Jerry.

Jerry agreed. The water below was as still as ice, but there was a strong breeze blowing across the natural skyway. Combined with the height, the narrow trail and lack of visible reference points, he was feeling like he was already falling over. A wave of nausea washed over him and he felt that he might lose his lunch... or at least his breakfast.

"How much farther before we get off this narrow ridge?" Bobby asked.

"I think it spreads out again over the next rise," Wizzle called up to him.

Once they reached a wide enough plateau to rest, they all slid down onto the ground. Their legs were rubbery after all the riding. CJ wandered over to the gear, unzipped his pack and pulled out his bag of cereal. This time Fink even tried a bit and smiled thankfully. Jerry dug out one of the packs of cheese crackers and a water bottle.

"So do you think they can catch up with us here?" Jerry asked

"Eventually, yes. But I don't believe they will even try," Wizzle answered.

"Why not?" CJ asked.

"They obviously know where we are going since they knew to wait for us back there. This route is much longer than the other, and if they are thinking at all, they will attempt to beat us to Crawford's Glenn."

"Crawford's Glenn?" CJ still did not seem to understand.

"Sure. This road will meet up again with the road they're on. It's a small village. Maybe six or seven gnome families live there. The other road is straighter, while this one twists and turns, following the shoreline as it scales the peaks and descends through the valleys. If they move on without stopping, they might reach the village where these roads meet before we get there."

"Then why are we just sitting here?" CJ asked, not even trying to hide the terror in his voice.

"The animals can't go on like this. They must rest after such a sprint," Wizzle replied.

"Where we come from, there is an old story they teach us as little kids." Bobby said. "It's called the Tortoise and the Hare. The basic idea is that a turtle and a rabbit have a race. The rabbit should win, right? Well, he's kinda arrogant. He runs for a while, looks over his shoulder and sees that the tortoise has just left the starting gate, so he decides that he has time to take a little nap. Of course, while he sleeps, the turtle strolls by and continues on to win the race. The turtle never strayed from his goal and moved on without pause. I'm just concerned that if we stop for too long or too often, that they'll get there first."

"Relax, Bobby. We have no illusions that we can stay put for any length of time and still beat them to the Glenn. But if we don't rest our animals, we may not make it there at all," Wizzle replied. "And while they rest, we should eat. There may not be another opportunity for a while."

As if on command, Fink waddled over to one of the gear-laden birds and removed a brown animal skin bag. He released the synch rope from around the top and started to remove some items. There was a large oval shaped package wrapped in paper, probably bread. After that came several dried fruits of different varieties like pineapple, papaya and bananas. There was some of the leftover cooked bacon from breakfast and some kind of large nuts. He did not bother to unpack the table, but spread out a blanket and distributed the food across it. The bread was dark and nutty and could have used some butter. It was pretty dry. There was still a bit of goat's milk that the native Tellusians shared, passing a single canteen around. Jerry shared his water bottle with the other two boys.

"So how long are we gonna stay here?" Bobby asked nervously.

"Eat up, and we'll move on as soon as we're full. I just wish there was some water here for them," Wizzle said, looking at the ostriches.

"Those guys back there really want us bad, don't they?" Jerry asked.

"Afraid so. Inar is probably terrified of what will happen if you boys make it to Neepol. I would be if I were him," Fink said.

"Jerry. In your premonition back there, did you see any bodies?" Wizzle asked.

He gave it a thought. "Yeah. Bobby. He was face down beside the road. Real bloody and no shoes on."

"Any others?"

"An ostrich, but I'm pretty sure that was it."

"Could you tell what happened to the rest of us?"

"I don't think I could. Why?"

"I was just wondering if Inar wanted you dead or alive. Or what he wanted with the rest of us, for that matter," Wizzle added.

"What difference does that make?" CJ asked.

"Maybe none, but it might be handy at some point to know his intentions," Wizzle replied. "If he wants you dead, they will be instructed to use any force necessary. If he wants you alive, they will have to be more careful not to hurt you too badly. If they are fighting carefully, we will be more likely to find a vulnerability."

Back on the trail, they kept their birds trotting at a pace that proved to be sustainable. The sun had moved across the sky in front of them and to the right. They seemed to be traveling in a southwest direction on the northern shore of the lake. The only stop they had made since lunch was for the birds to get a drink at a small pool of water by the side of the road. Wizzle had said that they should be to Crawford's Glenn shortly and sent the fairies ahead to scout for Inar's men.

"So what do we do if they're already there?" Bobby asked Wizzle.

"We will have to attempt to slip by unnoticed."

Sarcastically, he replied, "Oh yeah. They probably get lots of tourists loping through their little town on giant gray birds with giraffe necks!"

"Bobby!" Jerry snapped. "What is your problem?"

Bobby sighed and answered, "I don't know. I'm just scared I guess." Then to Wizzle, he said, "Sorry 'bout that. But I don't have any better ideas."

"It's alright, boy. We're all pretty edgy right now."

"Is there any way to maybe put them to sleep?" CJ asked. The rest of them looked at him funny. "I'm serious. Could Clairese put those Bigfoots under, or spike their drinks at dinner or something?"

The gnome thought on it for a few minutes. "I don't rightly know. We shall have to ask on their return."

"And if we do get there ahead of them, then what? We can't camp there, and if we continue ahead of them, our tracks on the road will give us away," Bobby said.

After a brief silence, Wizzle answered, "Perhaps we should split up. You know, ride off the road in the grass alone so as not to disturb the grass too badly. If we're lucky, the tracks won't be visible, and we can get back on the road on the other side of town."

Jacob and his sister zipped back into sight. They all stopped so that their collective guides could assess the situation. Clairese said, "They are about three kilometers behind us. We don't have to run to escape them, but it might be advisable. They are only walking; quickly, but just walking."

Wizzle instructed everyone on how to leave the fewest tracks by splitting up so no two travelers walked the same path, thus keeping the patterns more random and off of the dirt trail. He was a little concerned about leaving the scent behind, but regrettably, there was nothing they could do about it.

"If they get too close, is there a spell you could use to maybe put them to sleep?" Fink asked Jacob.

"No. They're still living creatures," Jacob answered. "We can't touch 'em."

"Okay. We ride now," Wizzle said, and they directed the ostriches to run. They did not ask the animals to sprint as fast as possible, but they were moving downhill at a good clip. When Crawford's Glenn came into sight, the fairies broke off again, heading over the hill to the right. The two gnomes and three boys with all their belongings in tow focused on the goal. All of them left the road, running in the grass on both sides now, chuffing along briskly.

Dropping into town, they all moved apart even more, darting between the houses and over the little stone walls. With no sign of their hunters, they raced out of the far side of town. About a hundred meters in front of them stood a rope bridge across the river that left the lake and ran south. Reaching the bridge, the river ran wild and deep below them.

"Oh. I don't know how I forgot about this," Wizzle said.

"Do we have to go across this thing?" CJ asked in a nervous voice.

"You betcha. And if we get out ahead of them, all the better."

"What about the ostriches?" Jerry asked. They were already backing away from the edge of the ravine.

"They're surefooted animals. Should be no problem for 'em," Wizzle answered back.

"But I get the feeling they really don't want to cross here," Jerry replied.

"Nonsense," Wizzle answered. "Fink. Show the boys how easy it is."

They were all yelling to hear each other over the noise of the rushing torrent below. The sun had slipped below the mountain-tops, though it was still light enough to see. Fink urged his bird forward, but it took two steps forward, and inched back.

"Come on, you," He said, trying again. He got the same response.

"I'm telling you. They're terrified," Jerry said.

"What do you mean, they're terrified? What makes you so sure?" Fink asked.

"Look, I just know, okay?" Jerry's intuitions were sending him stronger messages all the time. Each time that he suspected he knew what might be coming next, he was more sure of himself than before.

"Did they tell you they were scared?" Fink demanded indignantly.

"No...I can just feel it. Please believe me."

Fink still looked skeptical, but Wizzle asked, "So what are we supposed to do?"

No one had an answer, but Fink tried again more forcefully to coax his bird onto the bridge. Nothing doing. The giant fowl planted his feet and stood as if set in cement.

Finally, Bobby said, "On the farms where we come from, they teach you that you can't force a horse out of a burning barn. You have to put a sack over his head, or blindfold him somehow. Until you do that, he won't trust you to lead him out."

"Are you suggesting we blindfold the birds?" Wizzle asked.

Bobby nodded.

Wizzle sat thinking for a minute, and finally said, "What have we to lose? Fink, whatcha got over there that we can use for this?"

He coaxed the nearer pack ostrich to squat to the ground, and clambered onto the pile. After digging around a bit, he raised his arms with each of the boys' backpacks. With that Fink suggested they put on their coats. It was already getting cold outside anyway, and they could pack most of the other stuff elsewhere for the crossing. He had Jerry slip a backpack over his ostrich's head. He just stood there and let him do it. Then he gently started to lead the animal to the bridge. There was no resistance. He simply let Jerry walk him onto the rickety old swinging bridge. Jerry was terribly frightened, but would not allow that to get in the way of what must be done. Moving slowly so as not to spook the great bird, he finished crossing the bridge and removed the backpack from its head. He could feel the animal's sigh of relief from inside his own being somewhere, but there was no time to dwell on that right now. Bobby had already started onto the bridge with his ostrich and CJ had prepared his bird for the long walk as well.

Bobby was across and CJ was in the middle when Clairese returned with Jacob. They stopped to talk to Wizzle, but Jerry couldn't hear them over the rushing water below. Then Clairese flew over to Jerry. "Jerry, give me your bags. We have to get the rest of the animals across quickly. Inar's men are coming fast." He handed her his and Bobby's backpacks, and she levitated them over to the waiting gnomes. They prepared the pack animals first and Fink began to lead one of them across the old bridge. Jerry expected that at any moment, the boards on the bottom of the thing would break, sending man and bird to a rocky doom. It had not happened yet, but in the movies, it always happens to the last guy crossing. Wizzle started to lead the other pack animal across. When he was in the middle of the bridge, the ape-men appeared. They were still about two kilometers away, but that gap was going to dwindle fast.

Trying to hurry the bird across the ravine, Wizzle encouraged it to move more quickly, but it wasn't happening. The bird was still stepping slowly and carefully, making sure each foot was securely panted before lifting the next. The enemy moved closer. When at last Wizzle arrived on the other side, Jerry and Bobby sprinted to the other side to lead the last two birds to safety. The Sasquatches moved still closer. Finally, Bobby and Jerry each had one of the birds ready to cross.

"Go!" Bobby yelled at Jerry.

"No, you first," Jerry replied.

"Jerry, you're the one they want, now go."

"No. You first. I can close the distance much faster. We'll both get across more quickly if you go first."

Bobby didn't know that Jerry meant that he could 'talk' the bird across, but there was no time left to argue. He started his bird across the swinging bridge, while the attackers closed on Jerry. A gust of wind snatched Bobby's hat when he was in the middle of the bridge and flung it over the edge of the bridge. He grabbed at it in a futile effort to save it. The hat tumbled through the air, flashing the Philadelphia Eagles logo at him periodically. He only paused for a second. Now was not the time to mourn the loss of his treasured ball-cap. Jerry and the last ostrich stepped onto the bridge. Jerry and the bird stepped across at about the same rate the animal traveled on solid ground. As he reached the middle of the bridge, the gang of Sasquatch arrived at the other side. Getting ready to cross, they noticed Fink and Wizzle on the far side, one with an ax, and the other with a big knife. They halted, and in their defeat they watched helplessly as Jerry and the last animal reached the far side. In that moment, it became clear to all of them that Inar wanted Jerry alive. If not, the Sasquatch gang would have cut the bridge and let Jerry fall to his death. Once Jerry was on the ground again, the gnomes cut the ropes, and the bridge fell away.

"We can repair the bridge later for the local people," Clairese told Jerry. "For now, we just needed some distance between us and them."

No sooner had she spoken those words than a strange thing began happening on the other side. The gang of Bigfoot had huddled together for a short conference. Then they split up, and all but one of them moved away from the ravine. They lumbered toward the small cluster of homes in the Glenn and aimed their incinerators at the first one they came to.

"Send Jerry back here, or we torch the whole village, one house at a time," yelled the Sasquatch that stayed at the edge of the river facing them. It was the first time any of the boys had heard the real voice of their pursuers. He sounded to Jerry like a professional wrestler, jacked up with false bravado. He could not imagine stepping into a ring with the hulking thing, voluntarily or otherwise. Jerry looked in horror at the gargantuan creatures poised with their flamethrowers waiting for the order. He looked back to Wizzle. Wizzle stood fast, amazingly calm, then he open his mouth to holler back.

"The boy is going with us! Do what you feel you must, Knuruk, but you will have to one day answer for your crimes." With that, Wizzle climbed onto his ostrich, turned his back on the river and started to ride away. "Come along now, boys," he said in a quieter voice.

"You know him?" Jerry asked. He stood frozen beside his friends with disbelief. "Why didn't you tell us that before?"

"Wasn't sure 'til now. Knuruk the Red. He's second in command under Inar. Didn't really expect him to send out his top general for you, but I don't know why not. Must be pretty scared."

The three boys stood dumbfounded, shifting their gazes between Wizzle and the Sasquatches on the other bank, the roar of the river barely audible over the pounding of their hearts in their ears. CJ Implored, "We can't just leave those villagers to die, can we?"

"For now, Jerry's safety has to be our first priority. There is no more that we can do for them now," Wizzle said without any detectible emotion. "Besides, they'll probably be fine."

"10 seconds, dwarf." Knuruk the Red had given Wizzle a last chance to comply. Wizzle started to walk his ostrich forward, away from the river, without looking back.

After a silent eternity, Knuruk gave the command. "Burn it!" With yells and howls like Vikings berserking into battle, two of the Bigfoots savagely, even gleefully, set the first hut ablaze.

CHAPTER 10

Cheese Doodles for Breakfast?

JERRY, BOBBY AND CJ were still standing beside their ostriches, gaping in horror as the Bigfoot gang torched the third hut. If there had still been any question before as to whom the good guys and bad guys were, those thoughts had now been erased. Under no circumstances would the men with the white hats slaughter innocent people in their homes just to bring in their quarry, would they? Jerry glanced at CJ to find a tear running down his cheek. Bobby looked almost as stricken. He wondered how their guides could just march away like that. Couldn't they do *something*?

He turned to look at the gnomes, watching in disbelief as they strode away as if disinterested; like they didn't care at all. They stopped to talk with Jacob and Clairese who flitted near their heads. Clairese made a motion with her arms, pointing in the direction of the boys and Wizzle nodded. Then she flew over to Jerry and his friends.

When she had the attention of all three boys, she began, "Do you remember when Jacob and I were gone for a while this afternoon?"

They all looked at each other, thinking. "I guess so," Bobby said. Jerry was not so sure, but he had not been watching them carefully. He supposed that maybe he could recall something like that.

"We took it upon ourselves to warn the local villagers here in Crawford's Glenn that they were probably going to have visitors."

A glimmer of hope started to move across the boy's faces. "So, did they run off?" CJ asked.

"Not exactly," Clairese said. "We arranged a few surprises for their guests." A devious grin tugged at one end of her small mouth.

"Surprises?" Jerry asked.

She responded quite simply, "Just watch."

The houses continued to burn, but knowing they were uninhabited made the sight a little less sickening. Knuruk stood defiantly watching across the gorge at Jerry and his friends. He turned away and gave the command to set the fourth hut ablaze, and while his back was turned, the grass in front of his feet lifted up and swung quietly open like a door. While Knuruk's back was still turned to the new hole in the ground, six gnomes sprang from the cavity. In a blur of efficient motion, the first two gnomes wrapped a rope around the hairy giant's ankles and ran a stake into the ground that anchored his feet in place. Meanwhile, two of the other gnomes ran around to his left and two to his right. On each side, one of the little men held a rope with several stones on the ends, while the other carried a hammer and a wooden stake with a hook near its top. As it started to dawn on Knuruk that something was wrong, it was already too late for him to recover. He spun around and began to lose his balance. As his arms flung out to his sides in an attempt to regain it, the gnomes with the ropes let them fly, each one wrapping around one of the flailing arms with deadly precision. Like a massive tree, the Sasquatch started to topple. Knuruk let go of his incinerator as he opened his hand to break his backward fall. He called out for help, but his companions couldn't hear him. The fourth hut was a good distance away, and it was already engulfed in fire. The frenzied yelling and roaring flames drowned out all other sounds. He might as well have been alone at that point.

Crashing to the ground, the gnomes jerked the monster's arms above his head and with the ropes secured him to the ground before he could even twitch. Not having noticed that the first two gnomes had gone back into the hole in the ground, Jerry was surprised to see them emerge again with several more ropes and stakes. The ropes all appeared to have a loop in each end, and all six of the little guys set to work strapping him down. The entire operation took less than 20 seconds, and the gnomes vanished back into the hole in the ground, pulling the earthen door shut behind them.

The fourth hut continued to burn, and the rest of the Bigfoots never even looked in the direction of Knuruk. A moment or so later, one of the other plunderers suddenly started jumping around flinging his arms in all directions. Then another followed suit. Within only a few seconds, the whole lot of them were dancing and swinging their arms wildly about. It was as if they had gotten into a hornet's nest, and each one was running madly in his own direction, howling in panic. At first Jerry could not see the cause. The sun had disappeared a while ago, but in the dim twilight, the shadows danced as the flames illuminated the surroundings. Looking more carefully, he saw a gnome in the tall grass moving his arms quickly, but methodically. Surely, he thought, this one defender could not be the cause of all of this chaos. Looking around he spotted several others, and they all appeared to have slingshots with small balls.

"Zarches," Clairese said to Jerry.

"What?" he asked.

She answered, "Zarches. That's what the gnomes are using to fend off Knuruk's men."

"What's a zarch?" CJ asked from beside them.

"Those little things the gnomes are shooting at Knuruk and his men," She said. "They are somewhat like cockle-burrs. They're seeds from a plant that grows in the marshes near Nickarney. They're hard like wood, about the size of your thumb and have about 15 to 20 spikes protruding from each one. When launched from a schlinger, they can even penetrate a Sasquatches thick matted fur and painfully pierce the skin. Each point is barbed and naturally secretes a small amount of poison. It won't make anyone sick, but it stings like the dickens."

"Ouch!" Bobby said, after hearing the description. Jacob had just arrived from his conversations with Fink and Wizzle.

"So what's a schlinger?" CJ asked.

"I think it's one of those sling shot things," Said Bobby.

Then Jacob said, "It's simply a stick that branches in two different directions. Where the stick splits in two, there is a piece of rubber with a pocket built into it big enough to accommodate one of those nasty little zarches."

"Yep. It's a sling shot," Said Bobby smugly.

"You guys have rubber here?" CJ asked. "I thought that came from a factory." Jacob looked confused about what a factory might be, but Bobby explained that raw rubber actually came from a plant called a rubber tree.

Knuruk's men no longer even resembled a unit. They were running amuck. There was no organization as they ran hither and yon. Jerry was almost laughing at the show. It reminded him of some of the old slapstick movies he would watch on weekends with his dad. Bobby and CJ seemed to be enjoying the circus as well. As one of the Sasquatches neared a hidden gnome, he fell hard on his face as his feet became entangled in one of the ropes with the rocks on the ends. Three or four more of the little guys jumped out from unknown hiding places nearby and bound him as quickly as they had done with Knuruk. Again, none of the others seemed to be even remotely aware of the kidnapping that occurred in their midst. As the scene played itself out a few more times, Jerry was amazed at the precision with which the teams of little people defended their homes against the invading monsters.

Finally, there was only one left standing. He was jumping on one foot, trying to take a zarch out of his other foot when he fell onto his side and was swarmed by about fifteen gnomes. He never stood a chance.

Jerry found himself feeling sorry for the creatures tied to the ground. Immobilized as they were, they would not be able to extract the painful, spiked seeds from their own bodies and were at the mercy of the gnomes. Over the rush of the river below and the roar of the burning houses, the agonized wailing of the creatures left him with the feeling that he was looking at a battleground after a decisive skirmish, the land strewn with dying and wounded.

The amazing part to Jerry was that nobody had been killed or even seriously hurt, and he was sure that nobody would be. The Bigfoots had been ready to take the lives of the villagers. The locals were obviously opposed to killing, even though many would say they had a right to defend their homes to the death after such a brutal attack.

"So what happens now?" Jerry asked Clairese.

"We move on while they are detained," she answered. "The villagers will likely see to the wounds from the zarches on Knuruk's men and make sure they are fed 'til morning. That should give us plenty of time to move out of their reach, and travel in peace. Even when they are released, the next passage across the river is about 30 kilometers southwest. That should give us at least one additional day's head start."

"So, what do you use for a zarch wound?" Bobby asked.

"There is a fluid that comes from the Medicine Plant. Many people use it for burns, but it is also effective at easing the sting from a zarch," She answered.

"And what about their homes?" Jerry asked.

"Nothing that we can't undo," Clairese answered. "We should get moving. The more distance we can put between us and them, the safer we will be."

"Are there others? You know, on Inar and Knuruk's side?" CJ asked her.

"There are some, but without knowing what has transpired here, they may not be watching too carefully," Clairese replied. "Still. We will have to be cautious. They could be watching from anywhere."

The thought of countless invisible malicious eyes watching him made the hairs on the back of Jerry's neck prickle, and he had the sensation that there were monsters hiding behind every tree. Unfortunately, his parents could not be here with him to turn on the lights and chase the demons away. He knew he would just have to march into the face of his fear. There was no way to go back even if he had wanted to.

He glanced one last time across the small canyon. Three of the four homes were still burning, though the flames were beginning to expire. The first hut still had an eerie reddish glow emanating from the doors and windows, but the stone walls stood fast. The gnomes had split into two groups to care for the uncomfortable Bigfoots, but they were ignoring the last of the burning houses. As the thatched roof of the fourth burning house fell in, releasing a shower of sparks that rained up into the evening sky, Jerry mounted up and turned to follow Wizzle and Fink. CJ and Bobby did likewise, and none of them said a word as their birds began traveling again. When the boys caught up to their guides, Bobby was the one to ask if they would be traveling far in the dark.

"I expect it will be a little while before we make camp," Wizzle answered. They were riding up a steep grade toward the peak of a rocky hill. It was almost as dark as it would get, suggesting to Jerry that the time might be around 6:30. In his old life, he would have eaten dinner by this time, but mealtimes here would be determined by when it was safe to stop. He nudged Bobby, looking for some trail mix. There was a little left, which he shared with Jerry and CJ, but that was the last of it. Fink and Wizzle, who were couple steps ahead pretended not to notice that the boys were snacking and led them to the crest of the hill.

Before them lay the road they would follow south for the next few days. It was dark, but the moon, which was completely full tonight, blanketed the countryside in a silvery glow to the horizon. Looking at the landscape before him on clear, bright nights like this, Jerry could never understand how the moon could shine so intensely without generating any light of its own.

Wizzle broke the trance with a quiet announcement. "We are going to continue along this road a while. Jacob and Clairese will fly ahead to scout out a suitable campsite for the evening."

"How long do you think it will take?" CJ asked.

"Dunno," Wizzle answered. "We want to put some distance between us and Knuruk, but the temperatures really drop after dark this time of year."

"I thought they were tied up," Bobby said.

"Well, yes. They are. But you can never underestimate your opponent. It will surely be the end of you," Wizzle answered. "Remember watching them burn the huts in the Glenn?"

"Sure," said Bobby.

"At that moment, they looked unbeatable, didn't they?"

Bobby seemed to be really thinking this over. "I guess so," he answered finally. "But the Gnomes back there surprised them."

"Don't you think they could surprise *us*? Fortunes can change in an instant, and you can never, ever become too sure of victory; even when it seems to be in your hand," Wizzle finished.

Although he didn't like it, Bobby seemed to grasp the importance of what Wizzle was trying to convey. Jerry knew it too. No matter what they did, they would never be truly safe in Tellusia. All they could do is proceed cautiously and never take their luck for granted. He looked out again at the road ahead. In his head, he imagined that it was a giant game board, and he was just one of the players. Roll your dice, land on your square and hope the card you draw smiles upon you. In this game however, walking away was not an option when things didn't go the way you want them to. There were no do-overs, and there was no safety zone. This game would have to be played to the end, and winning was absolutely imperative. The fairies had already gone, and Fink and Wizzle had started down the hill. The boys again followed, as they had been doing since the night before.

After a few minutes, Clairese and Jacob returned with news of a clearing in a remote wooded area, probably about a half hour's ride south.

"It'll be about three or four minutes off of the road through the trees." Jacob told them. "There's a stream nearby for water for us and our animals. The path that runs through the clearing allows for an easy escape out of the back in case we are approached from the front, and it provides shelter from the winds, should any arise tonight."

As foretold by the small, winged siblings, the trees came into view. The road they were already on led directly into a leafless forest. The ghostly skeletons of the naked trees looked demonic, their shadows casting impossible black and silver mazes on the ground in the moonlight. There were some ground bushes and shrubby plants on the forest floor, but with the exception of a few ferns and rhododendrons, the ground cover was as lifeless as the canopy. Jerry began to develop the feeling that there was someone, or something, following them. He looked back, and of course, there was no one there.

Bobby called out, "Hey, is that the trail we want?" He was pointing to a path through the underbrush that looked like it was used by the local big-game animals.

"That's it," Answered Jacob. They all left the road and plodded into the forest. The temperature had dropped to the point that even the ostriches puffed out little clouds of vapor with each exhalation. Reflected in the light of the moon, each cloud had a supernatural glow, like little ghosts leading the way.

The clearing left Jerry breathless, like walking into a great cathedral. Everyone's eyes were drawn to the tops of the trees and the sky beyond. The moon and stars shone through the twisted branches like a heavenly light show. It was more beautiful than any manmade stained glass windows in the most ornate house of worship. The clear ground formed a perfect circle of silver-brown leaves and there were no other plants. The trail continued across the center of the clearing from front to back like the aisle between imaginary pews. It exited on the far side through a boulder that had split in two countless centuries ago, forming a natural alter.

Jerry was having a hard time defining the emotions that filled him. He could sense a paternal power beyond all others. He felt calm and safe, as if nothing evil could reach him here. Reaching into the inside pocket of his squall jacket, his fingers located the golden cross on a chain that he had found under a bench in the mall. He took it out and slipped it under his rugby shirt and around his neck.

After eating dinner by the light of the moon, they finished setting up camp and started to get ready to bed down. Again Jerry had that nagging sensation that they were being watched by someone just outside of their visible range.

"Wizzle," Jerry said. "Do you get the feeling that someone's spying on us?"

"Kid, it's felt like that to me since we got the assignment to come and collect you guys," He answered.

"No seriously. I'm certain of it. I can't see them, but I know they're out there."

"You know, I feel the same way." Bobby added, and he looked to CJ for agreement. CJ shrugged at Wizzle. But Jerry felt this on a more carnal level than any of the rest of them could understand.

"Well, maybe it would be best if we set up a schedule to post a watch," Fink suggested. "If there is someone out there, we might be able to get the jump on 'em."

Clairese had just come over to add her thoughts. "Well, how 'bout Jacob and I scout around a bit, just to see if we can spot anyone."

Wizzle looked to Bobby and Jerry and asked, "Do you boys suppose that would make you feel any better?"

CJ and Bobby nodded and Jerry went along with them, but inside he felt differently. If the fairies came back with the news that they saw no one, Jerry would be certain that they had just missed the trespassers. If, on the other hand they did spot any voyeurs, then they would have a new problem to deal with.

After Jacob and Clairese zipped off into the darkness, the remaining five travelers discussed a guard schedule. As they had no timepieces, estimates were the best they could come up with. The moon, which was almost overhead now, would travel the rest of the length of the sky well before dawn. Marking its progress across the heavens was the most predictable clock they had. Counting the fairies, there were seven of them altogether. They hoped to break camp shortly after sunrise, which was later in the winter than in summer, but would still feel very early to a troop who kept taking turns skipping an hour or more of their sleep.

"From that tree over there, we should be able to keep an eye over the entire camp and into the trees a ways." Bobby pointed to a tree at the edge of the clearing with branches low enough to grab hold of and climb easily, although Fink and Wizzle might find the distance between the branches a challenge due to they're miniaturized stature. "It is on the west, so the moon should be setting behind us keeping the glare out of our eyes when we're on duty."

Jerry thought Bobby sounded like a soldier, but that kind of mentality might be exactly what they needed to get through the night. "So who goes first?" He asked.

"One thing we will need to keep in mind is that for about two or three hours in the very early morning hours, it is going to get pretty dark. The moon will set tonight long before the sun comes up." Bobby said, a bit of uneasiness in his voice.

"Then the fairies should take those turns," Wizzle suggested. "They're night vision is far better than ours. And I'd wager it's better than yours, too," He added, looking at the three boys.

"Most likely," CJ agreed. "Once the moon goes down, I won't be able to see a thing."

"Why don't we draw sticks to pick the order? Everyone here will want to be first or last just so they can have an uninterrupted sleep," Wizzle said. They all looked at each other, nodding agreement. And so it was that they collected five sticks of different lengths and each one of them drew a stick from Wizzle's hand. Having drawn the shortest one, Fink would take the first watch, followed by Jerry, Bobby and then Wizzle. By then they guessed that it would be truly dark and Clairese and Jacob would have a go. Finally, CJ would get the last watch when the sun would begin to warm the horizon. Then he was to wake them all up as the top of the sun appeared in the east, assuming no one had sounded the alarm by then.

When their smallest comrades had returned to camp with the news that they seemed to be alone, the others heaved a sigh of relief while the good news did little to lift Jerry's spirits. Wizzle filled the fairies in on the plan for the night, and they were of course quite agreeable with the whole thing.

As soon as they were ready to settle in, Fink grabbed an extra blanket. He left his glowstone to heat the tent, and he headed up the tree. Once he managed to struggle up about 20 feet or so into it, he perched on a heavy limb that stuck almost straight out to the side where he would have to do the best he could to stay comfortable for the next hour. The rest of them made themselves as comfy as possible under the conditions, and settled in to sleep under the hypnotic pulsating yellow light.

Exhausted, Jerry was surprised to find that sleep did not come and take him immediately. He was still nagged by the feeling that something was hanging out, just waiting for the right moment to spring on them. When he finally did drift off, his sleep was light and agitated. He woke several times just in the first hour waiting for Fink to come and trade places with him, and felt even more tired than when he laid down to begin with. When he left the tent to assume his position in the lookout tower, Jerry was tired, but climbed with ease to the same branch Fink had occupied. The little man had left the blanket in the tree, so that Jerry would not have to lug one up there with him.

As his time passed at his post, his thoughts wandered to a lot of strange places. He thought about the day before his sister had lost her mobility. It had been a normal day. They had, as a regular family, gone to see a movie together. It was a happy memory though. They had a nice time together, laughing at the antics on the screen and sharing popcorn. Becca's wheelchair had not yet rolled into their lives yet, and the extra baggage of his mother's guilt was miles away. He considered how he had taken his family for granted, certain they would always be there for him. Even in the recent months while his family was planning to relocate, he had been considered in all of the decisions, although it was easier for him to resent them if he pretended they were ignoring his needs.

He thought back to Kyle, and how one afternoon they had been exploring a tunnel under the highway about a half a mile from the house. They had pretended they had found the hidden entrance into a pyramid, and found wealth beyond all their dreams. If only Kyle could see him now! The tunnel he had explored this time had taken him to places they could have never imagined.

He again considered his fellow travelers. It was looking as though his two new human friends were going to be the kind of friends he could count on all the time. But that birthday thing still kinda bugged him. How could it be that the three of them were born on exactly the same day? Exactly! He knew there was relevance there, but what was it?

His melancholy meandering was cut short when he heard the sharp snap of a twig on the far side of the clearing. The moon was behind him and shone only a short distance into the woods. There was nothing visible. Every nerve in his body had gone on high alert, reaching out to sense what might be out there, but all of his sensory input was coming back negative. Even with his squall jacket and the blanket wrapped over him, his skin washed over with waves of gooseflesh. After a time he came to question whether he had really heard anything, or if he had just made it all up in his mind. Unable to take it any longer, he descended from the tree, slipped as quietly as possible back to the tent to rouse Bobby.

The warmth in the tent was comforting, but Jerry almost didn't notice it. Bobby jumped and inhaled with a start when Jerry touched his shoulder. Looking up at Jerry with wild eyes, Bobby took a second or two to register where he was and why Jerry was waking him up. As he came around, Jerry ushered him silently from the tent to explain the new situation.

After Jerry laid out the scene, Bobby asked, "And you're sure that it wasn't some kind of small animal?"

"I'm not sure of anything. And I don't have any idea what it could have been," Jerry said. "But I am pretty sure that I heard *something*."

"Well, sometimes the woods just make noise at night. You know, worms, slugs, dew dripping from the leaves. That kind of stuff," Bobby suggested trying to comfort his friend, but the nervousness in his voice cancelled out his intended conviction.

"Not in November," Jerry responded.

After a brief pause, Bobby conceded, "No. Not in November. So what do you think?"

"I don't think I want to stay out here alone. Will you sit up with me for the rest of my watch, and I'll stay with you for yours?" Jerry suggested.

"Yeah. Okay," Bobby answered, with a tired smile to show his support, and the two boys scaled the tree to keep watch over the rest of the sleepers below. They made themselves at home and sat quietly for a while.

"So this whole thing is pretty freaky, huh?" Bobby whispered, finally breaking the silence, but not looking at Jerry.

"Yeah," Jerry agreed. "Pretty freaky."

"Do you think we'll ever get back home?"

"Right now I would just settle for living a few more days."

"I know what you mean," Bobby answered. "Have you ever been able to see things in your mind before?"

Jerry considered for a moment how to answer this one, but finally decided that if they were going to be on the same team, he could not be keeping any big secrets. "Yeah, a few times. Usually right before something major is about to happen."

Jerry explained about the time when he saw his sister tumble down the stairs and about the deer that his aunt almost hit. Bobby listened, amazed. Finally he asked, "So can you control it? Like, can you feel or sense what's about to happen right now?"

He answered with a prompt "No." He had never tried to direct this ability before, but pondered whether it was even possible. He closed his eyes, trying to feel if there was anything important about to happen. After several minutes with no result, he gave up. The only things that even crossed his mind were images from Saturday morning cartoons. He saw a picture of a dog eating French fries. He also saw those two crows that smoked their cigars while they heckled the other characters. It was all nonsense.

"I didn't see anything," Jerry finally answered. "Well. I did, but they were just cartoons."

"You got any favorites?"

"Well, I don't watch a lot of 'em any more, but I do still love the superhero cartoons. You know, Superman, Spiderman, stuff like that," Jerry said. "How 'bout you?"

"I'm a Looney Toons guy, myself. Hanna Barbera. Daffy kills me, you know. Especially when he mixes it up with Bugs." Bobby said.

"Yeah. In one of those, it might be Tom and Jerry, there's an old black woman who stands on a stool, swinging a broom at a mouse. When will she ever learn?"

"CJ's mom is black, you know?" Bobby asked.

Jerry was stunned by the abrupt change in topic. "Well, I didn't mean anything by that."

"Yeah, I know. But I just thought you should be aware. It's not the kind of thing I would just blurt out in front of CJ. Might be kinda rude," Bobby said.

"Oh."

"Well, for one thing, did you realize that January 15th was the day Martin Luther King, Jr. was born?"

"Yeah. I think I remember hearing that before."

"I mention it because it's an important part of who he is. The January 15th birthday thing we all share is strange, alright, but in his house, Martin Luther King is like a superhero. You know, able to leap tall color barriers in a single bound... Anyway, CJ and I have been friends from day one, and a lot of times, we go places together. You know, I might go out to dinner with his family, or he might go to the mall with mine. That sort of thing."

"Okay. Sounds normal enough."

"That's just that point. It's totally normal to us. When I was in second grade, though, I started to notice that people stared at his parents. And at us. Not everyone, but enough to make me uncomfortable. That's when I realized that the whole mixed-race thing wasn't normal to everybody else. Eventually, I stopped noticing. Anyway, it shouldn't change the way you feel about him, but I think it's important."

"Why's that?"

"Just is. It's who he is, and since you haven't met his family yet, you wouldn't have known that. You might pick it up in conversation, but it's not the sort of thing that he would just say without a reason. He grew up in that home, and I think he forgets that his family is in any way different from others."

"But it's not, is it?"

"Only in appearance. But to some people that's a lot more important than the real difference."

"What's that?"

"His identity is mixed up with all that family heritage stuff. Where most kids like to see Grandma once in a while, he lives for the time he gets to spend with his extended family. Most kids were tucked into bed listening to Dr. Seuss. CJ's family shared stories about their ancestors. He says, that's how they keep them alive. In a lot of homes, there are, I don't know, um, a bunch of people living separate lives under one roof. In CJ's home, there's a close knit family sharing their lives together."

One of the ostriches made a sneezing sound, and the boys jumped, but it didn't make another sound. The rest of the watch was quiet, and when they figured their time was up, the two of them headed down to wake Wizzle. The moon was already moving down toward the horizon, and morning would be on them before they knew it. Sleep had to be the most important priority so that they could be at the top of their game tomorrow.

Jerry and Bobby told Wizzle about the last couple hours, including the breaking twig and how the two of them teamed up to spend a double watch together. Wizzle bade them goodnight, and left the tent to take his turn aloft. The boys tucked under their blankets in the toasty tent. They exchanged a look that acknowledged their camaraderie, even brotherhood. Then they rolled over and went to sleep.

As the sunlight danced across the top edge of the tent, Jerry awoke to the sound of sniffing and scratching. As it worked its way around the shelter, Jerry crept out of his bag and peered through the opening of the tent into the treetop to see where the lookout was. There was CJ, wrapped in the blanket some 20 feet or more off the ground, asleep. The noise outside the tent had stopped, but Jerry knew that whatever had been making the sounds was still there. He just could not decide if it was friend or foe. Just as he started to turn to wake Wizzle, a splash of red and gray burst past the entrance. Intrigued, Jerry looked back out the door again and found himself face to face with a dog wearing a red bandanna around its neck. It had patches of black and brown around his face and some dirty white hair covered the rest of his head. The main part of his body was mostly speckled light black and tan. A black ring around his tail gave him a decidedly beagleish look when viewed in conjunction with his face, but he was bigger than any beagle Jerry had seen before, looking to be about the same build as his aunt's Border collie, Molly.

From nowhere in particular, Jerry heard a voice. He was sure it was the 'voice' of the animal staring in at him, but by intuition alone. Prior knowledge told him that dogs don't talk. It was not in his head, and it did not seem to come directly from the dog either, but there was no question that Spot was addressing him. And the beast wanted something.

The dog's request was simple. "Hey, Dude. You got some cheese doodles or something? Like, I'm *starvin'*!"

CHAPTER 11

Rudy Kingman

FORTUNATELY FOR Jacob and Clairese, they had chosen to make a perch in the top of the tent, secured to the center pole that supported the whole thing. This was lucky only because if they had been sleeping on the floor, they might have been crushed in the confusion that descended instantly upon the entire crew as a shocked Jerry fell backwards into the tent and wiped out the offending pole! They had however been jarred from their beds and had then toppled on to the top of the writhing mass of bodies and blankets, each of them wrestling to free themselves from the squirming pile. Before anyone rolled on top of them, each of the fairies had flown out to the edges of the collapsed tent. The boys and the gnomes were all talking at once, in a befuddled assortment of protestations.

Outside of the tent, CJ could be heard shouting something about a dog, "He's going that way!" Piled together under yards of limp canvass, no one could possibly have known which way the dog ran because they could not actually see CJ.

Jerry was trying to catch his breath. The others all looked expectantly at him.

Not feeling very patient, Bobby urged him, "Well? What the heck was that all about?"

Before Jerry could answer, CJ burst through the tent opening and yelled, "The dog... he went... back into... the woods over... there." Pointing to his left, he was winded from his sprint down the tree and across the clearing. Judging by the dirty scuffs on his jacket, face and hands, his descent from the tree had not been graceful.

Several inquisitive eyes turned back to Jerry. Finally, he found his voice. "A dog was sniffing around the tent door."

"Yeah, so?" Bobby interrupted.

"Let him finish," Wizzle said, looking gently at Bobby. Meanwhile, he and Fink started working to prop the center pole back up to support the roof of the tent.

"He spoke to me," Jerry said. They all stared at him. He detected a combination of faith and disbelief at the same time from his friends.

"What do you mean, *he spoke to you*?" Bobby prodded.

"Just that. He kinda... well, his mouth didn't move, but I heard him clear as day!" Jerry said. "He was looking for food."

"Any kind of food in particular?" CJ mused.

"Actually, yes. He asked for cheese doodles!" The two other boys laughed and Jerry joined in after a moment. The others looked lost. They didn't see what was so funny.

"What are cheese doodles?" Fink asked.

"They are a snack food back where we come from." CJ answered. "Why?"

"We've never heard of them." Wizzle answered for the other gnome.

All at once, Jerry realized the implication of that statement. "So where would that animal ever have heard of them before now if you can't get them here?"

"A different realm," Wizzle answered him. The other two boys understood immediately.

"He must have followed us," Bobby said quickly.

"He could have never gotten across the chasm at Crawford's Glenn," Wizzle noted.

"So how else would he have gotten here?" CJ asked. He had made his way into the tent and was sitting on the ground now.

'There are many gateways that we know about, and I'm sure there even more that we don't," Wizzle answered. "The possibilities are endless,"

"Should we look for that poor creature?" Clairese inquired of Wizzle.

"Yes, I think so." He turned to CJ and asked, "Did you see where he went?"

"Not really. He was running away pretty fast, into the woods, and I was just trying to get you guys up before anything else happened."

"Else?" Bobby asked. "Why what did you see?"

"That's just it. I fell asleep up there. I didn't see a thing before I heard Jerry holler. As I woke up I saw this gray blur tearing off across the clearing. I tried to call out to you guys, but it looked like you were in trouble here. The tent was bouncing around and it sounded almost like there was a fight in here, so I tried to get here as soon as I could. By the time I reached the ground, the dog was gone."

"Which way son?" Wizzle asked in a paternal voice. CJ had already told them the direction, but things were still pretty confused at that point, and he wanted to be sure. CJ pointed again in the direction the animal had run, and the fairies departed in search of him.

When Wizzle lifted the tent flap to let Clairese and Jacob out, the sunlight poured across Bobby's face. "CJ?" He asked.

"Yeah?"

"How long were you asleep up there?"

"I don't know. Why?" CJ answered.

"'Cuase it's full daylight out there."

"Sorry." CJ responded.

Wizzle turned back to Jerry and asked, "Can you remember exactly what he said to you?"

"The dog?"

"Yes."

Jerry considered this for a moment, then he answered slowly in a monotone voice. "It was something like *Hey Dude. Like, I'm starving. You got some cheese doodles or something?*"

"I don't know anyone back in Pee-Ay that talks like that." CJ said, using his hometown slang term for Pennsylvania.

"Hey, that's a good point," Bobby agreed.

"Maybe he's from a city. You know, like New York or something." Jerry suggested.

"I don't know," Bobby interjected. "Sounds like some of the high school kids that hang out in the neighborhood at night."

"That could be," CJ said. "Maybe he fell down the same well we came through."

"Wizzle's right. I don't think he could have followed us across the river back there," Bobby reminded him. "But, here's the important thing. Do you think he was here as a friend or an enemy?"

"I don't think he wanted to hurt us, but I really don't have any way to know for sure. I was mostly still asleep," Jerry answered. They all seemed to think on that; it got quiet, and no one had anything left to say.

The fairies had returned with news that the dog had vanished as quickly as he had appeared earlier. They began to get ready for the day ahead, changing, eating and packing up camp. Once the birds were loaded down with their baggage, the miniature caravan got underway again.

Back on the main road, they continued south. The night before, the path had looked snow covered in the silver moonlight. Today, the mixture of light sandy soil and white stones crunched under the feet of the great birds as they trotted briskly along. In turn, each of them looked back from time to time to see if the canine was following them, but there was no sign of him. By midday they had left the forest behind, and were out in the open hills. If their visitor had been pursuing them, he would not have had an easy time of staying covered.

During a water break for the ostriches, Jerry again started to develop the feeling that they were being stalked. His friends took him more seriously this time, but still failed to share in his sense of alarm.

"Last night you thought we were being tailed, and it turned out to be a skittish dog," Bobby noted. "Maybe our next encounter will be with something equally as frightening."

"We should hope to be so lucky," Wizzle commented. "But not everyone out here will be our friend, Bobby."

"I know, but I can't go on spending all of my time scared and looking in all directions, watching for the next attack."

"You can, and you must," Wizzle responded. "Fear is a funny thing. Sometimes, your fear will lead you to a place where the very thing you are most afraid of will come to pass. And we are all afraid of something, but many of us learn to be brave in spite of it, lest we live only half a life because we're hiding from those things that scare us."

"So are you telling me not to be afraid?" Bobby asked.

"Not at all. What I am saying is that you must learn to live like you are not afraid. Shaymalon wisely says that courage is not the absence of fear, but the ability to persevere in the face of it."

Sarcastically, Bobby said, "Boy, I can't wait to meet this guy. He's just full of great stuff."

Wizzle glanced to Jerry, who just shook his head as if to say *Don't worry about it.*

As the sun started to reach for the horizon, Fink and Wizzle had explained to the boys that they would be staying with an Ogre who was sympathetic to their cause. He lived in a cave outside of a town called Gloxny. "His name's Kingman; Rudy Kingman. Not too bright, but he's a good man. He's been helping out the oppressed for years," Said Wizzle.

"Once returning home in a terrible blizzard, he came across an injured Gnome left by the side of a frozen stream," Wizzle continued. "Turns out, he had been beaten by a couple of Inar's men and left to die in the storm. Matter of fact, he was taking some correspondence to the gnomes in Crawford's Glenn about a coming raid that they had learned about back in Amosbury, near the Great Stone Calendar, Stonehenge. They were..."

Bobby cut him off. "Stonehenge?" He asked excitedly. "That exists here? I thought that it was only where we came from."

"Oh no, boy. Among other things, it was once used by many visitors as a gathering place, and it's been used as a calendar by several different civilizations. One exists in all the realms, not just Earth and Tellusia." Wizzle sounded almost insulted.

"All? How many are there?" CJ asked.

Wizzle looked at Fink, and there was a short silence while only the sound of the ostrich's feet scuffling on the dirt could be heard. Then Fink answered thoughtfully, "Don't really know. But there are at least 15 or 20."

All three boys looked in awe, and even the fairies seemed surprised by this bit of information.

"Probably even more than that," Wizzle added. "See, that only accounts for the ones on *this* planet. You add in all the other planets that the original architects traveled to, and it could be hundreds, maybe more than a thousand. Who knows?"

"So you can travel to other planets?" CJ asked him.

"No. Not really. That gateway is hidden. It's been lost to us for thousands of years," Wizzle answered.

"Oh this is sooo wild," CJ exclaimed. "And all this time, NASA has been trying to find faster ways to get to other worlds, when they should just be searching for that gateway." He was obviously getting excited. "You know, they launched the Voyager probes almost 30 years ago, and they are just now leaving the solar system. On a map of the known universe, our entire *galaxy* would be smaller than a pin prick on the side of a barn!"

"I don't think the Omnicrons came from your *known* universe," Wizzle cut in.

All three boys looked like they just missed something. Jerry asked, "Who are the Omnicrons?"

"That was what the original architects called themselves," Wizzle replied.

"And how can they come from beyond the universe. I thought that was a term we used to refer to... well, everything." Bobby stated.

"Think bigger, Bobby. Think *much* bigger. Two days ago, your universe only existed in one place and one time, right? Your place and your time. Today, you should be able to see that there are many places and times existing simultaneously."

CJ suddenly looked like he was going to explode with excitement. "I get it! I get it! Think of it like this. If the entire collection of universes is like a box full of spiders where each spider represents a specific universe or time thread or realm or whatever, and they are all making webs in the box, the webs are going to cross each other all over the place. In some places they might even touch! Those would be the gateways, right? ... where they connect. So, each spider would make a web for his own reality, and each web would be specific to that spider."

"That's an excellent model," Wizzle said. "And fairly accurate. The Omnicrons are a far advanced race, and they managed to connect those webs in places to use to their advantage, and to everyone else's advantage for that matter. Once they made the connections, they could travel the length of the known universe in a second or two, and between times as effortlessly. And finally, they could move between any time and place and realm in a single step."

"And the spider box model has another interesting dimension to it," Fink added. "There is almost no end to how many more webs can be added. And to how many connections can be made between them."

"So are these Omnicrons Gods or something?" Bobby asked.

"I don't think so. I think they were just given a certain responsibility in the Big Picture. We Gnomes have our place, you have yours, and they have theirs. We will never know what the plan is until we are done and get a chance to look back over it from beyond."

Jerry's head was getting that *too much information* feeling again. Wanting to get the subject back to something smaller, he asked, "So what is this stone hinge?"

"Stonehenge," Bobby corrected him with a laugh. "It's an ancient ruin in southern England, built before man kept written records of what he was doing. It is a ring of stones that stand up straight with other giant stones piled on top. Scientists think it might have been used as a calendar and for religious ceremonies. Really though, there is as much mystery surrounding it as there is around the pyramids. We don't *really* know who built it, or exactly how it was used or what the original builders were thinking. Think about it. They lifted these stones in the air after dragging them for miles - huge blocks of solid bluestone that weighed 20 or 30 tons each - and stacked them on top of other monstrous stone pillars. How did they do it? And why was it so important? If the labor came from local people, they would have had to leave their farms for years. Why would whole villages of people risk starvation to pile up a few rocks?"

"They didn't build it," Wizzle said.

"The Omnicrons?" CJ mused.

"Yes. And a race that can reorder the universe as they can would probably be able to build one of these things with very little effort," Wizzle answered.

"So why are there Stonehenges in every realm? What are they really used for, I mean?" Jerry asked.

"We think they might be the primary gateway points that the Omnicrons used in attaching this realm to the interuniversal network," Wizzle answered.

"But you just said it was lost," Bobby said.

"Yes I did. If Stonehenge is the primary gateway, no one here knows how to get it to take them off the planet. Either we were never shown how to use it, or the ways have just been forgotten. Regardless, it will get us to Inzia."

Narrowing the topic down even more, Jerry inquired about the travel time from the Inzia gateway exit until they would meet with Shaymalon.

"Not too long after we pass through. It's another 800 kilometers, but it will go a bit quicker. You boys don't have any problem with heights do you?" Wizzle asked. Fink shot Jerry a sideways glance. It made him uncomfortable.

"What do you mean fear of heights," Jerry asked.

"Shaymalon has arranged for a different kind of bird to meet us at the portal," Fink said, still grinning.

"Different?" CJ inquired.

"It's a *big* bird, a bit like an eagle," Wizzle answered.

Fink burst out laughing. "Yeah. You know. Like the dinosaurs were big lizards!"

"Oh stop that!" Clairese said to Fink. "We're probably meeting a Great Golden Hawk there for the last leg of the trip to Neepol."

"Right," Wizzle confirmed. "You'll be glad you brought your jackets. It gets kinda cold up there."

"So how high are we going?" CJ asked.

"Let's just say that you won't want to fall out," Wizzle answered.

"And it's just a day in the air? How long 'til we get to Amosbury and Stonehenge?" Bobby asked.

"With luck, tomorrow night. We should be getting to Kingman's place in another half hour or so. There we can get our bearings, and figure out tomorrow's plans," Wizzle said.

"Cool. I was really starting to get hungry," Bobby replied.

The feeling of being watched swept over Jerry like a huge wave from nowhere. He jerked around to look over his shoulder, but there was nothing in sight that should have been causing the sensation. Conversation abruptly stopped as the others turned around to see what Jerry was looking at. Wizzle and Clairese exchanged a worried look and she left to investigate.

"It's alright boy. We'll move on to shelter, and she can keep an eye out." Wizzle said. Then, turning to Jacob, he asked, "Would you keep watch from above?" Jacob nodded and went instantly aloft.

"No one will be able to approach without warning here. It's too open on these rolling fields, and they can't come up on us without being seen; especially with Jacob's eyes above," Wizzle said to the boys.

Jerry was almost shaking with anxiety. "I don't care what they find or don't find. I'm telling you. We are not alone."

"If there's someone watching at this point, one of the fairies will find them." Fink responded.

"Fink! They didn't see the dog in the woods last night," Jerry barked back.

"It was dark," Wizzle said calmly.

"But you said they can see in the dark," Jerry snapped.

"No. I said they can see *better* in the dark than we can. And at night, the dog could have gotten lost in the shadows."

"And what about this morning when he ran off. They never found him then," They didn't seem to get it. He didn't just think they were being watched, he *knew* it.

Clairese returned empty handed from the north, and Jacob was coming in fast. "Clairese. Clairese. Come quick, the crows," He shouted in his biggest little voice. Everybody's eyes turned skyward in unison, and they all searched for signs of birds above them. Nothing. The fairy siblings rocketed back up and out of sight.

Finally, CJ said, "There. I think I see them," He pointed almost straight up. Sure enough, two black specs were headed away from them on high. They were so high, it was hard to be certain if they really saw them. Everyone pulled up on their reigns and watched as the birds continued to move farther away. Even the ostriches seemed to be taking the spectacle in. All at once, the crows were flying in random directions, swooping and dodging some invisible attacker. Apparently, Clairese and Jacob were making things difficult for the them. Wizzle interrupted the silence by reminding everyone that they needed to continue.

"Quickly, ride while you can. We've been seen. I suspect those birds are some of Inar's minions," Wizzle urged his ostrich to move, and the rest of them followed, more urgently than before. When Jerry looked up again, the crows were much easier to see. Jacob and Clairese must have been forcing them down. With the ostriches in a heavy trot, they were covering a lot of ground in a hurry. Finally, they could begin to hear the crows' protests and the fairies were even visible.

When the evil black birds were at last on the ground, the group of riders approached cautiously. Wizzle dismounted and walked up to the crows and demanded of them. "Who are you? Give me your names, right now!"

"I'm. Caw... Caw... Algernon. Caw... My wife. Caw... Yesplenda," The crow answered.

"Why are you watching us?" He asked.

The one called Algernon answered him. "Caw... Caw... Please don't hurt. Caw... Inar. Caw... Took fledglings. Caw... Caw... We are slaves. Caw... Caw." Jerry could feel the bird's pain, and wanted to mend it somehow. As he had seen so many times in his comic books, the *monsters* were just misunderstood. The birds weren't evil; just parents trying to do the best they could for their kids.

"Whoa. Do all the crows talk here?" CJ asked.

"No. Crows can be trained to talk. Inar probably had his tongue split," Fink said.

"Had their tongues split?" Bobby asked back.

"Sure. If you slice a crow's tongue down the center, it can be taught to speak," Wizzle answered.

"So what are we going to do with them now? Cut their tongues *out*?" Jerry asked. "We can't let them go. They'll go right back to Inar, and who could blame 'em."

They thought for a moment, and CJ suggested that maybe the fairies could use some kind of magic to wipe their memories.

"Sorry. We can't do anything like that." Clairese said. "Our powers are restricted to the non-living."

"What about the tree you tossed at the Sasquatches? You can use 'em on plants?" Bobby asked.

"No. It was dead," Jacob answered. More silence. The crows were looking nervous.

"Wait," CJ said. "How did you force these two down here if you can't use those powers on living things?"

"We can move the air," Clairese answered. "We didn't do anything *directly* to the birds, we just blew currents up that made it impossible for them to fly."

"Cool." CJ said.

"I've got it," Jerry snapped. "Back in Maple Lake, where I used to live, there was a bird sanctuary. Some of the bigger birds living there were injured and being nursed back to health. One of the veterinarians there told me once that if a bird was in danger of leaving before it finished recovering, they would clip a couple of feathers."

"Caw... Caw... Not my flight feathers! Caw..." The female crow pleaded.

"I'm sorry ma'am. It would be in the best interest of all Tellusia," Wizzle explained. "If you can't return, you can't be forced to talk to him. And Inar won't be able to jeopardize our safety. You can come with us to Rudy Kingman's cave for the evening. He may be able to keep you safe and fed until your feathers grow back."

"But, Caw... Caw... Our fledglings? Caw..." Algernon protested.

"There is no way of knowing if they're even alive now, or maybe Inar's pressed them into service, too," Wizzle said evenly. "Inar is not an honorable man."

Yesplenda's grief was obvious. She hung her head and didn't make a sound. Instead, she just shook. Algernon moved closer to her to offer comfort, but it was too much for Jerry. He had to look away, allowing them their dignity. Wizzle told the crows that they would have to come along to Rudy's place, but not to try escape in the meantime. The crows assured them they would do as they were told then hopped and flapped up onto the pack ostriches for the remainder of the day's trek.

The moon was already out when they arrived at Rudy Kingman's cave and a hot, red sun was just settling into the western hillside for the night. Jerry had been expecting Kingman to live in a cave hollowed out from rock, but this looked more like a hole dug into the side of an earthen mound. There was an opening above the doorway where the smoke exited from the fire burning in the middle of the room. Next to the fire there was a stout, almost portly, green-skinned bald man. Even his hands had the swollen look that many infants have. He was roasting a dog sized animal over the fire pit. As they poked their heads in the entrance, Rudy's face lit up and he jumped to his feet. He had to be seven or eight feet tall. "By Jove! If it isn't Wizzle Saunders and Fink Meyers. It's been ages," he said, embracing the little fellows. His voice was big, full and jovial.

"And you've brought some friends," Kingman looked out past the Gnomes and spied the three boys in the crowd. "One of you must be Jerry."

"Yes sir. That's me," Jerry said, and he slid off his ostrich to approach the ogre. If they had not been standing under a canopy of rich green foliage, there was no doubt that Kingman's shadow could have covered all three boys at once.

"Well, it's an honor to meet you, boy," Rudy said and held out his hand. When Jerry reached up to shake, half of his arm was swallowed by the ogre's immense, green hand. "I've heard a lot about you. We're expecting big things from you and your friends here. Big things."

"Yes sir," Jerry said, not really sure what else to say.

"So. Which one of ya's CJ?" Kingman asked to other two boys.

CJ tentatively put his hand up.

"Come on down here, son. Don't be shy. We're all friends here." Kingman bellowed. He took a step closer to the boy who was climbing down from his ostrich and swallowed the boy's forearm in his grip. "Thrilled to meet you, boy. Just thrilled!" Then he looked at Bobby like he was a long lost brother, and just said, "Bobby, right?"

"Yeah," Bobby said. Before he could dismount, Kingman strode over to him in two huge steps to shake hands. The rest of them made their introductions. The ostriches were penned up with a couple pigs and a few goats. In the next pen, a half dozen enormous sheep munched disinterestedly at a mound of hay. Jerry found himself absently staring at one of the sheep before it dawned over him that it had two heads, one on each end. As he became aware of what he was looking at, other oddities began to work their way into his head.

Running around on the ground, in and out of the enclosures without a care, were chicken-like creatures with heads like frilled lizards, complete with the fantastic plumage around their necks. A medium sized cage to one side of the cave door housed a rabbit... with two antlers protruding out of his head. *A jack-a-lope?* Jerry thought. Kyle's father had had a jack-a-lope head mounted on a plaque, but Jerry had been sure that it was a practical joke, not a real animal. Maybe it wasn't such a joke after all.

Rudy fought to get the boys' attention away from the strange livestock and ushered them all inside. Crowding through the door, Jerry found that there were not a lot of places to sit, and some of the smoke from the fire hung above his head near the ceiling. Fink and Wizzle climbed up onto a hollowed out windowsill, with the fairies beside them. The crows moved close to the fire pit, and all but drooled over the meat cooking there. The boys found seats wherever they could, either at the table with Kingman or on the floor.

"So, tell me how the lot of you came to be traveling together," Rudy said to anyone who would answer.

Wizzle spoke up. "Shaymalon sent us to meet the boys, so we..."

"Shaymalon, huh? So how's he getting' on these days?" Rudy asked.

"Very well, actually. Sharp as ever and he doesn't look a day over 700," Fink answered. The men laughed.

"Good. Good. He's a good man! It'll be a sad day when he's gone, eh?" Kingman said.

"Yes it will," Wizzle answered. "I hope I don't live to see it."

"So, we met the boys back in Nathan's Cavern and took 'em topside, where some of Inar's cronies had wrecked the camp. That's when we met up with these two and the rest of their family." Wizzle gestured to Clairese and Jacob. "They found us a safe place to make camp and get a late dinner."

"If you knew our mom, you'd know that she puts on quite a spread. There was enough to feed a small army," Jacob added.

"It was a right good feast, to be sure," Wizzle agreed. "Anyway, Mrs. McKlesky sent these two little ones along." He nodded at Clairese and Jacob. "They've already pulled us out of a couple close shaves."

"You expect me to believe that two great gnomes like yourselves needed someone else's help?" Rudy asked, laughing.

"Yeah. Strange, I know." Wizzle responded. "As a mater of fact, they brought Yesplenda and Algernon down to talk with us."

"Caw... He's got our little ones. Caw... Caw..." Algernon said.

"You mean Inar?" Rudy asked. "He's a right, bloody treat, idn't he?"

"Yeah. He's taken the crow's kids. Told them that if they ever wanted to see 'em alive again, they would have to, you know, do a little spy work," Wizzle said.

"Caw... Caw... If we don't, caw... tell him where you are. Caw... Caw... Kill the kids. Caw..." Yesplenda pleaded.

"We'll do what we can for your children, ma'am," Jerry heard himself say. Then to Yesplenda, he said again, "There are no guarantees, ma'am, but if we do ever come across your children, we will do what we can for them."

"Rudy," Wizzle said. "Do you mind if we leave these two here with you for a while? We just can't take them along."

"You can, caw... trust us." Algernon said.

"I'm sorry sir, but if my children were being held hostage by that monster, the only thing you could trust me to do is whatever it took to get them back. And if I thought that turning Jerry in would do that, I fear that I would do exactly that," Wizzle said.

The crows moved together in silence, heads hung down again. Jerry understood. They all understood.

"Sure they can stay." Rudy said finally. "It'll be a spot warmer in here than traveling along with that crew. I'll tell ya that."

"Thanks, Rudy," Fink said. "So whatcha got to eat around here?"

"Little bit of bush deer. Couple a' wolves took it down right across the field over there," Rudy said, gesturing out of the door. "You know me. Someone's gonna d'liver dinner to me doorstep, I'm gonna eat it. I'll just grab a few more sweet potatoes from the pantry and drop 'em in the coals for ya."

"You stole that from some hungry wolves?" Bobby asked in disbelief.

"Yeah. Sent the little buggers yelpin' home to mommy, I did," Kingman said with a chortle.

While Rudy Kingman tended to dinner, the rest of them laid out blankets and got ready for a welcome night's sleep. Wizzle had asked Bobby to borrow his pocketknife, and with some help from Rudy, clipped two feathers from the tips of each of the crows' wings. While there was no physical pain, the poor birds were terrified about how they might get on without being able to fly. Rudy assured them he would look after them, but without flight, Algernon complained that they were cutting away the birds' very identity.

Soon, they were all huddled around the fire. Rudy cut hunks of cooked meat from the carcass above the fire, and passed out the sweet potatoes.

"So how far do you suppose it is to Amosbury?" Fink asked with a leg bone in one hand and a fork in the other.

"With them leggy birds you got penned up out there, probably about a full day's ride if you get started early enough," Kingman answered.

"Do you remember the last time we were here?" Wizzle asked Mr. Kingman.

"Sure do. You were with that other guy. What was his name?" Rudy asked.

"You mean Stringer?"

"Yeah, that's him. How's he doin' these days?"

"I expect he's got it a bit easier than we do. He's working in the Displaced Species Relocation Department now. When they bring some poor creature over from the other side, he works to help 'em get a new home over here. Not easy, but a heck of site safer than working for The Coalition." Wizzle said.

"What's The Coalition?" Bobby asked.

"The Tellusian Freedom Coalition. It's a group of us who believe that the oppressed peoples of Tellusia should have a voice," Wizzle answered. "Inar would love to have us out of his way."

"And you're that voice?" CJ asked.

"Well, we try. Just as in your realm, sometimes you have to be willing to fight for what's right. When you see a great injustice, you can't just stand by and let it happen," Wizzle said.

"You mean like Inar enslaving the birds?" Jerry asked.

"Blimey. He's got more den just a few of them birds enslaved. In da mines he's got..." Rudy started to say.

"Mines?" Bobby asked.

"Rudy, you got any more of those ribs over there?" Wizzle asked.

"Sure do."

"Who's in the mines?" Bobby blurted out, refusing to let the subject change.

"A bunch..." Rudy started again.

"Rudy, stop. We've been asked not to discuss this in front of the boys," Wizzle snapped.

"Why in blazes not?" Rudy asked.

"Shaymalon wants to explain it to them, himself," Wizzle answered.

"Seems a right spotty thing to do. Don'cha think they have a right?" Rudy said.

"What I think is not the issue here," Wizzle said.

"Well he may have told you to keep *your* trap shut, but he never said nutin' like that to me." Rudy started to turn to Bobby.

"Kingman, could I have a word with you alone?" Wizzle asked.

Rudy Kingman stared disbelievingly at the gnome, then stood slowly and turned to the door. Wizzle followed him outside and the two men stepped just out of earshot. The room was filled with an awkward silence. The boys had been so close to getting some answers and were again denied the story.

To no one in particular, Bobby said, "Why won't anyone tell us what's going on?"

Clairese answered quietly. "Shaymalon is a great man. He can see many things, and he has true wisdom. We just have to trust his motives."

"Trust him?" Bobby spat. "How in the heck am I supposed to trust him? I've never even met the man and he's keeping secrets from me!"

"Then trust *me*," She said gently.

"Oh man, I want to. But it seems like this secret's a big one, and I'm just a little frightened. Okay?" Bobby replied.

"Yeah... It's a big one," She answered, looking away.

Bobby finally let it drop, shaking his head in defeat.

Jerry had pieced a bit more together, and wanted to tell Bobby and CJ what he thought, but would have to wait until the boys were alone together.

When Wizzle and Rudy came back in, the ogre looked like one more person with a big secret, but also like someone who wanted to tell his secret to the world. Jerry was sure that, given the chance, Bobby would try pry that information out of him.

CHAPTER 12

The Big Kahuna

THE NEXT MORNING found them mostly warm and dry. They were inside Rudy Kingman's hovel beside the dying embers of last night's fire, but the cool November air rolled across the floor from outside. A heavy fog was swirling in through the window hole and under the door. When Jerry awoke, he found that only CJ was already up.

CJ whispered to Jerry, "Man, I keep hoping to wake up in my own bed."

"Yeah. I know. I never thought I would say it out loud, but I miss my mom," Jerry admitted.

"Me too," CJ answered, a pool of clear liquid forming across his bottom eyelids. "It's Monday, you know? She likes to watch me get on the bus each morning from the house. Somehow, it's just one of those things. Like she misses me when I'm gone. This must be tearin' her up."

"My mom probably doesn't even notice I'm gone," Jerry said.

"Oh. You know she does," CJ said.

"I know. But Becca's her favorite. Ever since the accident, it's like I almost don't exist."

"What accident?"

"It was a couple years ago. She was being pretty snotty, but my mom lost her temper. She was gonna hit Rebecca, but when she started to swing out, my sister jumped back and fell down the stairs. Now she's probably gonna be stuck in that wheelchair for the rest of her life and my mom feels like it's her fault."

"That doesn't sound like she's your mom's favorite. It sounds like she just feels bad and wishes she could fix it, like maybe she feels like she needs to earn your sister's forgiveness," CJ said.

"Yeah. Well it hurts. Okay? I've kinda been ripped off here," Jerry said back. "Anyway. Doesn't matter much. We're probably never gonna see our folks again. So she can have Rebecca, and I've got you guys."

"Oh, thanks." CJ had a sound of mock disappointment in his voice.

Bobby made a guttural slurging noise, then a long exhale as he stirred a bit in his sleep.

"You know what I mean," Jerry said.

"Yeah. But look, *you* might want to stay here forever, but I'm planning to get back home as soon as I can," CJ said. "In the meantime, we can't afford to feel sorry for ourselves. We are going to have to focus all our energy on getting through this thing so we can find our way back."

Jerry agreed, then he lay back down for a few minutes. He got back up on one elbow and looked at CJ again. "How long have you known Bobby?"

"As long as I can remember, I guess. Why?" CJ said.

"Don't you think it's weird that we all have the same birthday?"

"Yeah. I've been thinking a lot about that. When we were little, we hardly noticed. Then it began to seem kinda cool. For the last couple years, we had a skate party at the rink for both of us together."

"Bobby pointed out that Martin Luther King, Jr. was born on the same day." Jerry stated.

"Yeah."

"I've been trying to put the pieces together, and I think we're in for a heck of a ride."

"But what does Martin Luther King have to do with any of this?" CJ asked.

"Maybe everything," Jerry answered. "He was a great civil rights leader, right?"

"Yeah. So?"

"Think about it, CJ. Wizzle and Fink talk about destiny. They knew we were coming before we got here, and that we're supposed to lead them out of some sort of bondage."

Wizzle started to stir, but slept on.

Then in a quieter voice Jerry continued, "Mr. Kingman said something last night about slaves in Inar's mines when Wizzle cut him off."

A look of quiet terror moved across CJ's face as he grasped what Jerry was telling him. "Oh. No way... I mean, really. No... Oh, this can't be right."

Across the room, Rudy Kingman bellowed out a great screeching yawn, waking the rest of them up at once. CJ and Jerry were looking at Bobby as if to say, *Man. Have we got some news for you... but it's gonna have to wait.*

"You guys been up long?" Bobby asked.

"Just a few minutes," CJ told him.

Bobby sat up, rubbed the sleep from his eyes, then stood up and walked to the door. He slipped outside for a moment, then returned.

"It's pretty foggy out there," Bobby said. "Clear sky though, I think. But maybe a little warmer."

Rudy went to the fire pit, stirred it up a bit and dropped a handful of smaller sticks onto the embers. They burst into flames at once, then he added a couple of smaller logs. He took some of the left over bush deer meat, and set it on a few sticks beside the fire to reheat.

The boys put their clothes back on, and to Jerry's dismay, he found that he was starting to smell pretty funky. To the other two boys he said, "Well, this'll be day four in the same outfit with no shower, and my clothes are starting to stink."

"Yeah, mine too," Bobby said. He looked over his shoulder and said, "Hey Jacob. You got some kind of magic spell that you could use to make us all smell nice and pretty again?"

"Sure," the fairy answered. "That's an easy one."

"No, wait. I was just joking." Bobby said to him, alarmed, but it was too late. Jacob had already spread his arms wide and closed his eyes. Bobby's clothes started to glow and a second later it was over.

"WHOA!" Bobby exclaimed. "I don't think I'll ever get used to that... that deep warming sensation. It was just like that portal... sorta. Anyway, my clothes feel like they just came out of the wash." He stuck his nose into his armpit and took a long sniff and crinkled up his face. "I think I could still use a shower though."

"We can restore things to their original condition, but we're not allowed to touch a living creature with the power. It's an ethical thing, really. I guess if we tried hard enough, we could get around it, but it goes back at least a hundred generations in our kind. It would be pretty hard to turn against that kind of history," Jacob explained again. "The clothes I can make new again. You... You're on your own."

Jerry looked at CJ and CJ nodded back. "Could you do us too?" Jerry asked Jacob. A moment later, Jerry and CJ stood in brand new clothes.

At the table, Rudy had placed a stack of plates, some knives and forks, and some hunks of deer meat. He took a pitcher from the shelf beside the window and went outside. Algernon and Yesplenda had already hopped upon the table and were pecking and tugging at a steak-like piece together. When the boys got there, there were only a few smaller pieces left, but everyone shared what remained.

Mr. Kingman came back in and set the pitcher on the table. "Sorapian Sheep's milk." He said. He got a handful of glasses down from the same shelf as the pitcher and set them on the table. Bobby poured himself about a half glass, but CJ held back, curling his lip up at the yellowish beverage. Jerry poured himself a small amount of the sheep's milk as well. He took a small sip, and gagged a bit. It was warm, and tasted thick and sweet.

"Can you pass the water?" CJ said to Fink at the other end of the table.

Jerry felt the sudden and overwhelming need to excuse himself from the table and walked outside. Mostly, he just needed to use the bathroom. He forgot to leave the rib bone he had been gnawing on at his plate, and set it on a tree stump. He stepped into Rudy's outhouse to take care of business. As he exited the outdoor waterless closet, he turned to grab his breakfast and froze to the spot. Through the morning mist, a brown, black and white dog with a red bandanna was sneaking up on Jerry's rib bone. They locked eyes for a moment, then Jerry slowly reached down and picked up the bone.

The voice of the dog was again crystal clear when he addressed Jerry. "Du-u-ude. How 'bout you throw the nice doggy a bone?"

"Nice doggy, huh? You scared me silly yesterday morning, then ran off."

"Yeah. Sorry 'bout that. But you were actin' kinda sketchy, man," the dog answered.

"Sketchy? Well it's not everyday that dogs just come up and talk to me."

"Oh, man. We talk to everyone we meet. But you dudes just never listen."

"Don't listen! That's got nothing to do with it. I've just never heard a dog talk before, if that's what you would call this." Jerry was not quite yelling.

"I don't know what else you'd call it. But you're, like, the first human's ever made any sense."

"Maybe that's because people can't talk to dogs like this!" Jerry answered back.

"Like, you seem to be doin' just fine."

"Yeah, well. This is just too weird."

"You want weird? Used to be, the guys I lived with did some of the strangest things."

"Oh, yeah? Like what?"

"Like, I would say something like *I gotta go outside to pee,* and they would throw me a piece of pizza! Or I would ask if we could go down to the beach, and one of them would let me out into the backyard. Man, it was, like, fenced in. How lame is that?"

Jerry thought about this for a minute. He thought about how tough his life would be if no one understood a word he said. He thought about the guys the dog used to live with. And he thought about...

"Hey dog. What's your name?"

"They call me Kahuna."

"Kahuna, huh? Where you from?"

"San Marina, California. It's like, near the boardwalk, ya know."

"Kinda warm there, isn't it?"

"No. It's nice there. It's kinda like, freezin' here!"

"Look. If I give you this bone, you gonna run off? I mean, I think there's more inside."

"Man. You got food and, like dude, I am your best buuud." The dog replied.

Jerry tossed him the bone, and the dog snatched it from the air, dropped to the ground and started gnawing away.

"So how did you get here from California?" Jerry asked the dog.

"Dunno, really." Kahuna didn't even have to stop chewing to answer.

He probably knows, but just doesn't want to tell me, Jerry thought.

"No, I really don't know," Kahuna said.

Jerry snapped to attention, and stared at the dog. "Can you hear what I'm thinking?"

"Uh, yeah." The dog said *Yeah,* but to Jerry it sounded like *Duh,* as if this should have been evident all along.

"So, you were living in California one minute, and the next minute you're here. How long you been here?"

"Since the night before last," Kahuna answered.

"So what *do* you know about how you ended up here?" Jerry prodded him.

"Well, the last thing I remember was charging that wave, then it gets like all foggy, and next thing I know, I'm lying on the side of a river. Now I'm thinkin' to myself that I must be in dog heaven - at least I hope it's heaven - and I'm wonderin' what happened to the dude on the surf board."

"What dude on the surf board?" Jerry asked.

"The one I went after. My owner dudes were lifeguards on the beach, and some guy on a long board disappeared for a few minutes after he got creamed by this killer wave. Anyway, Slash jumps down from his chair, rockets into the water, and I follow him. We get out a ways from the shore, and I get caught in a rip. I'm getting' dragged under, swirling and spinning and tumbling, and I think, like this is it. Say goodnight Susie. I'm comin' home. Ya know what I mean? Next thing I know, poof, here I am. I'm cold and wet, and it's kinda dark down in this canyon. So I shake off. I'm pretty good at that. I can getcha wet from like, six or seven feet away, no prob."

"Not bad," Jerry agreed.

"Yeah. It always makes Slash and Jimmy yell at me to stop. I know they think I can't understand 'em, so I just go right on shakin'. Drives 'em nuts, ya know. So, I'm, like down by the river, and I look up, and there's a bunch of guys walking these giant birds across a bridge upstream, and I'm barkin' and barkin', then some guy's hat falls into the river near me. Then some little guys cut the bridge loose. I guess they couldn't hear me, 'cause no one even looked my way. I think they were talking to someone on the other side. Anyway, next thing I know, I'm alone again, but I start to smell smoke. The smoke starts drifting across the canyon like huge clouds and I think to myself, *Kahuna,* that's what I call myself, ya know; *Kahuna, you better get outta here. It's not safe.* So I run downstream a while and I find this trail going up one side. Before I know it I'm, like, on the top lookin' down, and I can see in the distance these houses smokin'. Looks like they were burned down, and I'm kinda glad they're on the *other* side of the river."

"Yeah. We were the guys crossing the bridge with the big birds - ostriches - and I think you came up on the right side of the river. Those houses were torched by some bad dudes," Jerry said to Kahuna.

"Meat's gone. Got any more?" Kahuna asked.

"What?"

"This bone's spent, dude. You said there might be more meat if I hung around."

"Oh... Yeah. I think so." Jerry turned to go back into Kingman's cave, and at that moment Fink stepped out.

"Jerry, you okay out...?" Fink stopped talking when he saw the dog. "Well, looks like we have a visitor," he said finally.

"Fink, this is Kahuna. He's the one that spooked me yesterday morning."

"Kahuna, eh?"

"Yeah. He's definitely a friend, but he's real hungry. Is there any more to eat in there?" Jerry asked.

"You'll have to check with Rudy. The meat on the serving plate is gone," Fink said.

"Bummer," Said Kahuna.

"No. Don't say that. It's okay. I'm sure we can find something for you," Jerry said to the dog.

"What?" Fink asked.

"I was telling him that we would find him something," Jerry said to Fink.

"There may not be much," Fink said. "Maybe he could pick through the bones that we were gonna toss out."

"Cool. That would be awesome!" Kahuna exclaimed.

"He said that sounds great," Jerry told Fink, who gave him a strange look, like he wasn't sure he heard him right.

"He *said*?" Fink asked. "You mean he spoke to you?"

"Yeah. He told me... Oh yeah. You can't hear him can you?" Jerry asked Fink.

"I can hear you, but that's a dog. They don't talk," Fink said.

"Tell ya what, kid," Kahuna said. "If the little guy's gonna give you a hard time about this, I could just snack on *him*."

"KAHUNA!" Jerry snapped. "Fink's our friend. You can't..."

"Jerry, what is your problem?" Fink asked.

"The dog says that if you're going to give me a hard time," He paused to consider what he was going to say. If he told Fink what Kahuna really said, the gnome would never trust the dog. "He says... that maybe he should just go and find his own food... ah... in the pig pen."

"That is NOT what I said," Kahuna said.

"Quiet!" Jerry hissed at the dog.

"Jerry, that dog didn't say a word," Fink said. He was starting to become annoyed.

"Well, no. Not out loud." He thought for a moment, then said, "Maybe I can prove it to you."

"You don't have..." Fink started to say.

Jerry turned to the dog and said, "Do something unusual, but tell me what you're gonna do before you do it."

Kahuna answered, "Okay. Tell him I'm gonna come over and bite his cute little hand off."

"NO!"

"How 'bout I, like, snatch that stupid, pointed cone off his head?"

"Kahuna, knock it off!"

"Alright. Alright. Um, how about if I walk in a figure eight around you two, then, um, I'll, ah, pick up a stick from behind you and put it at his feet."

"Sounds great," Jerry answered, a bit exasperated. He explained to Fink what was about to happen, and gave the dog a nod.

The canine looked up at Jerry for a moment then said, "This is kinda humiliating, you know?"

"It'll be okay," Jerry assured him. Kahuna got up on all fours started to walk between them, then around behind Fink. In a mocking form, he exaggerated every movement, as if he was walking on a high wire. From behind the gnome, the dog gestured towards Fink's hat in a mock snapping motion with his jaw. Jerry fixed him with a sharp look, and Kahuna continued on his path. He came back around and between them again and finally around Jerry. Then he turned behind himself, found a small stick by Rudy's woodpile, carried it over and laid it at Fink's feet. He looked back over his shoulder for approval from Jerry, who was beaming.

"Well, I'll be..." Fink said, fingering his long gray beard. Then to Jerry he said, "Are you sure he's safe."

"Yeah. He's alright."

Fink sighed and said, "Yeah. I think there might be some deer bones inside that he can chew on a while. But I don't think he's going to find 'em real satisfying. We picked 'em pretty clean."

"Woo-hoo! Sign me up, Jack!" Kahuna said and he moved a couple steps closer to Fink, looking to be petted on the head. He was a medium sized dog, but looked Fink in the eye, and the gnome appeared to be uncomfortable. Still, Fink reached out tentatively, scratched the dog on the side of his neck and pulled his hand back.

"Oh he's so cute I just could eat him up." Kahuna imparted to Jerry in his best grandmotherly tone. Jerry just glared at him, and was glad that Fink didn't see the look.

Fink turned back to the door and pulled it open. He called inside, "We have another guest Rudy. Hope you don't mind." Jerry followed Fink through the doorway, with Kahuna right behind him. The dog's eyes instantly locked on Rudy Kingman, and his hackles bristled. Everyone else heard the canine growl, but Jerry just heard, "Holy Guaca*mo*le! That guy is uuug-ly! I'll bet it's a good thing I'm color blind, ‘cause he don't look like he feels too good either."

Jerry did the best he could to ignore what Kahuna was saying and tried to calm him down. "It's okay, boy. He's alright," he said in that voice that even grown-ups use on dogs and little kids. As the animal started to relax a bit, Jerry added, "It's alright Kahuna. Good boy."

"Where did he come from?" Bobby asked excitedly.

"The river valley back in Crawford's Glenn." Jerry explained. "It seems he was trying to help rescue a drowning surfer in California and got dragged into another portal that dropped him by the riverside."

Bobby made eye contact with Kahuna and held a leg bone down where the dog could see it. Kahuna looked up at Jerry and didn't have to say a thing. Jerry nodded. Kahuna walked over and took the bone from Bobby's hand. He got the bonus treatment, a very meaty bone with the ever-popular scratch behind the ears.

"Oh man, this is good," Jerry heard the dog say.

"His name's Kahuna," Jerry stated. "He used to live with a couple of beach lifeguards. I think he's kinda homesick."

"Yeah. I know how that feels," CJ said.

"Me too," Bobby agreed.

"I'm not so much homesick," Kahuna said. "More like food-sick. Man, those dudes fed me all the time. Good stuff, too. Cold pizza, cookies, chips and the occasional beer in the water bowl on Friday night."

Jerry glanced distastefully at the animal. "I don't suppose you could keep your thoughts to yourself?"

"What did *I* say?" The dog answered with a mock tone of innocence.

"So he followed us all day?" CJ asked.

"Yeah. And the last two nights," Jerry answered. "Sounds like he arrived here in Tellusia when we were crossing the rope bridge back in Crawford's Glenn."

"Did you feel him coming this morning?" Bobby asked.

Jerry looked thoughtful for a moment, and then said that he had not.

"Why do you think that you could sense him yesterday, but not today?" Bobby asked him.

"I don't know," said Jerry. That question left all of them thinking quietly for a moment.

"Maybe he can only feel a malicious or threatening presence," Wizzle suggested.

"But Jerry said the dog is okay. Why yesterday and not today?" Bobby asked again.

"Maybe he wasn't sensing the dog last night. Maybe someone else was nearby last night." Wizzle said.

Jerry could almost see the light bulb come on over Fink's head. The gnome turned to Algernon. "When did you first start to follow us?" He asked the crow.

"Caw... Caw... Cawford's Glenn. Caw..." Algernon answered.

"That explains that," Wizzle said. "Were you in the trees last night?"

Both crows' heads bobbed up and down.

"Okay," Wizzle said.

The travelers finished eating, packed up and made ready to move out. Some of the fog had started to burn off, but the sky above was so clear and blue that it almost shimmered.

"Dude, where we goin' now?" Kahuna asked Jerry.

"To Amosbury."

"Like, where's that?"

"A long way. You can probably stay here with Rudy," Jerry said.

"Yeah, right. He's kinda freaky lookin' if you ask me. And you know, in some cultures, they eat dogs," Kahuna said.

"Oh, come off it," Jerry said. "If it weren't for him, you'd be scratchin' for roots right now."

"Yeah. You're probably right. He's probably just trying to *fatten me up*!"

"You've got quite an attitude, don't ya?" Jerry asked him. "Did those guys you lived with treat you badly?"

Wizzle called, "Jerry, let's go. We gotta long way to go today."

"Alright." Jerry climbed up onto his ostrich. Wizzle started to lead them away from Rudy Kingman's home and back towards the road. He called good-bye to the ogre.

"Cheerio, boys," Rudy said, then, "Oh yeah. You too Clairese."

She smiled, waved back to him and called, "It's okay Rudy. I hope to see you again real soon."

CHAPTER 13

Thunderhoof

THEY FOLLOWED Wizzle out, with Fink taking up the rear.

"Oh no, doggy. You stay here with the nice ogre," Fink said when the dog trotted by.

Ignoring the gnome, Kahuna ran up beside Jerry and pleaded with him. "Look, I don't even know where you're goin', but you gotta let me come. I can't stay with that dude. He, like, gives me the willies."

"Sorry. But I think you give Fink the willies," Jerry answered him. "Maybe if you hadn't looked so hungrily at him earlier, he wouldn't be so intimidated."

"Dude, you can't make me stay here, you know? I'll follow, and he can't stop me."

"No, but Fink and Wizzle can decide not to feed you," Jerry said. "Look, if it were up to me, you could come along. Even with your attitude, I think you're kinda cool."

"What attitude?" Kahuna answered back sarcastically.

"Yeah. That one."

"Look man. You gotta take me along. I can't stay with Mr. Freak-n-stein here, and I'll starve out there alone."

"So what am I supposed to say to Fink? I don't think he trusts you."

"Look, Jerry. I'm not a bad dog. I would never, like, eat the little guy. He looks too old and chewy."

"See, that's what I'm talkin' about. It's comments like that..."

"Okay. Okay. I'll try to behave myself," Kahuna pleaded. "What do you need me to do?"

"You're gonna have to convince Fink that you really don't want to eat him. Heck, it probably wouldn't hurt if you could explain how helpful you want to be?"

"Like, what makes you think I wanna help him I the first place?" Kahuna asked.

"For one thing, you're hungry. And if we all work together, there should be more than enough food for everyone." Jerry said. He stopped beside the dog and managed direct eye contact, then he added, "And if you weren't the helpful kind of dog, you would have never gone fishing for that drowning surfer. I think you act tough so that no one can get close, but it gets kinda lonely living like that."

"Alright. You caught me. It's all a bluff. I don't want to hurt those little guys. Heck, I couldn't. I just like to joke around, that's all."

"I know," Jerry said to him. "And that's great, really. We could use a laugh or two. But we have to make sure that we can prove to the gnomes that it's just a joke."

Fink's ostrich pulled up beside Jerry and the dog. The gnome glared at the canine as he strode by, and gave Jerry a glance that said *leave him and get going.*

"See. He hates me," Kahuna said.

"Look. When I first met Fink, I thought he was a bit shifty, not particularly trustworthy. But when he warms up to you, he's okay. If you wanna come along, were gonna have to persuade him. I think Wizzle's already cool with the idea."

After a thoughtful pause, the dog conceded that he'd better try to talk with Fink. "Okay. Will you tell Fink that I want a truce?"

"You sure 'bout that?"

"Yeah."

"Okay." Jerry cantered up to Fink and asked him if he would talk with Kahuna for a moment.

Fink nodded begrudgingly, then added, "But I'm not promising anything."

Jerry signaled to the dog, who walked with trepidation over to the pair on the ostriches. Jerry explained to Kahuna that he was going to tell Fink every word he said, so he had best not joke about things like snacking on uncooperative gnomes. Kahuna agreed to the terms of the negotiations and set out to argue his case while Jerry translated. Jerry was impressed.

Kahuna started out with a sincere apology for his bad behavior upon meeting Fink. He explained that it was just in his nature to be a smart aleck, but he didn't mean any of it. Then, to his surprise, Jerry heard himself passing on some really selfless reasons why the dog should join them on their trek.

"He says dogs naturally protect the people they call their friends and they have a nose that can detect danger well before the people around them can," Jerry imparted to Fink. "And he says that his sense of smell would, like, come in handy when you're lookin' for food."

Fink hadn't said a word. He just listened. He sat quietly on his ostrich, thinking. "Alright," He said finally. "He can come along for now. But, Jerry, if he even looks at me funny, he's outta here."

Kahuna's tail wagged so hard that the animal was flexing back and forth from the middle of his torso. "Woo-hoo! I'm coming along. Yeah baby! Yeah baby!" Then it hit him. "Hey. So where *are* we going? I mean, after we get to... Amosburg?"

"Amosbury." Jerry corrected him. He explained the trip the best he could. He was so engrossed in it that he hadn't even noticed that they had walked up out of the fog until they crested a hill and the landscape spread out in front them. Before him, the hills rolled on; frost on the trees sparkled gloriously in the early morning sunlight. The thing that really moved Jerry most was the way that the fog settled into a twisting valley for miles in front of him like an enormous puffy serpent. CJ and Bobby had both reigned in their birds and took in the view.

"Why does it look like that?" Jerry asked the other two boys.

"It's a river," Bobby answered. "The water temperature is a bit warmer than the air, so the steam rises off it, and the cold air keeps it down in the trough."

"Wow. It looks amazing," CJ said.

Bobby noticed Kahuna standing beside them, and looked at Jerry. "Daddy said we could keep him?"

"Yeah." Jerry answered with a light snicker. "I don't think Fink's too thrilled with the idea, but he'll come around. Kahuna says that he'll earn his keep, and I think that's what finally pushed Fink off the fence onto our side."

"Well, I think it's great," CJ said. "He seems like a nice dog."

"Oh man. He's cool! I have to admit though, it's still kinda weird to hear the dog's voice, especially when he's chewing on something. It reminds me of those ventriloquists. You know? The ones who drink a glass of water while the puppet sits on his lap and chatters away."

"I can't even imagine," Bobby said to him. "But then, *everything* is kinda freaky. Each morning I wake up and keep my eyes pinched shut 'cause I'm hoping I'll wake up in my own room. But I know it's real, and I don't wanna see."

"Yeah. It's kinda like summer camp," CJ said.

"It's *nothing* like summer camp! For one thing, I don't remember wearing a winter jacket to camp." Bobby was almost shouting. "In summer camp, you get up, you have breakfast, you go on a nature hike, ya have lunch. Then you play a little volleyball, go for a swim, have dinner, roast marshmallows and go to bed. I don't remember anything about risking your life all day long or saving the world in an alternate reality at Camp Sing-Song!"

"Well... yeah. There's that," CJ conceded. He removed his Flyers hat and, holding the brim of it in his hand, used it to scratch an itch on top of his head. "But you know what I mean. Sleeping in tents, eating food cooked over a fire, spending all day outside. Bobby, you gotta chill out."

To CJ, Jerry said, "I know what he means. I'm kinda scared too. But it's cool too, this whole adventure thing."

Jerry heard Kahuna say, "I kinda miss the French fries under the boardwalk, and chasing those squawking seagulls."

"Yeah. Some fries would be real nice right now," Jerry agreed, and the boys trotted on again to catch up with the rest of their group. Jerry's ostrich pitched forward, perhaps tripping over a rock or a hole. But as he felt the impending fall, certain that he was going to be tossed like a sack of bird seed onto the ground, he shouted out the first thing that came to mind.

"Oh, FUDGE!"

"Where?" The dog perked up. Jerry's ostrich was already beginning to regain its balance.

"Not where. What!" Jerry said.

"What?" CJ asked, not realizing that Jerry had been addressing the dog.

"Huh?" He had managed to stay aboard the staggering bird, but Jerry was now caught up in a flashback. It was a memory from another lifetime of sitting on the sofa with his father on a Sunday afternoon watching old black and white slapstick TV shows. "Awww. Wiseguy, eh?" The lines rolled through Jerry's head while he saw the old program in slow-motion.

He had thought a lot of his mother and sister since arriving here, but hadn't given his dad much consideration. It hurt Jerry to think about him too much. He wasn't home very often. Mom said he worked a lot. He did of course, but there was more to it than that.

He used to spend a lot of his time with his father, but that was before Becca's accident. After that, his dad spent more and more time at "the office." His mother pretended not to notice, but Jerry knew the truth. With increasing frequency, his dad was stopping off at the bar for a few drinks on the way home. Usually, he stayed until late at night, not having dinner with his family or even seeing them before bed. Sometimes at night he could hear his father stumble in, knocking things to the floor. Occasionally the man would vomit in the downstairs bathroom. On many nights, if Jerry went to the bathroom in the early morning hours, the smell of stale beer would waft out of his parents' bedroom, greeting him like a foul intruder in the hallway.

Yes, Jerry knew the truth. His father was in pain, big time pain. He was trying to deal with Rebecca's difficulties by drinking reality away with beer and whiskey. It broke Jerry's heart and he longed to have his old father back. Maybe one day he would return home. Then, at least have his new father back. That would be the most he could dream to hope for right now.

By midday, Kahuna had disappeared several times to get a drink or chase a squirrel, or whatever it is that dogs do when no one's watching them. One of Kahuna's more amusing exploits of the morning was when he chased a Killdeer around for about ten minutes, repeatedly calling, "Get back here, you crazy chicken."

But the Killdeer was on her own mission. She was running about, dragging one wing on the ground, pretending it was broken. That was how she kept her nest safe. She lead away whatever predator might have been interested in her nest by looking like an easy victim. When her assailant got too close, she would fly just out of reach, and start the charade all over again. Finally the dog just gave up, and Jerry heard him say something about how the bird wasn't worth his time. Now, Jerry heard Kahuna complaining again, before the dog was even in sight.

"Man. I could really be diggin' on a taco right about now. I'd even eat the lettuce," Kahuna whined. "When's lunch, dude?" Then, he held his nose to the breeze, and ran off to the side of the road. Having traveled so far south, many of the trees here still had some brightly colored leaves hanging on them, which swirled to the ground each time the slightest breeze kicked up. Kahuna rooted around until he found what he was looking for, then he started eating it.

"Man. What are you eating, now?" Jerry asked him.

"I think it's a dead rabbit," Kahuna answered, ripping into the smelly carcass. "Think it's been here a while. It's got a nasty aftertaste."

"Oh. You are so gross," Jerry said back to him.

"What do you mean?"

Jerry gave an exasperated sigh, then called, "CJ. You still got that bag of cereal in your pack?"

"Oh. Yeah. I forgot all about that." He trotted over to the ostrich that was carrying his backpack. What he found was a bag of cereal crumbs, and he held it up to show the other boys.

Jerry and Bobby looked at the squashed bag that CJ clutched, and they grinned. "It looks like some settling has occurred," Bobby exclaimed, and the three of them laughed heartily for a moment.

"I don't get it," Kahuna said.

"That's what it always says on the cereal boxes," Jerry explained to the dog. "You get this big box of air with a little food inside, and the cereal company prints that on the box so you don't feel like you're being ripped off so bad." The other boys still felt kinda uncomfortable when Jerry talked to the dog like this. He imagined it must be like listening to half of a phone conversation.

"So, either of you guys want any of this stuff?" CJ asked.

"Nah."

"No, thanks."

CJ dumped the contents of the bag onto the ground. Kahuna carried the dead rabbit over to the pile of cereal crumbs, dropped it on the ground and inhaled the heap of cereal pulp in seconds.

"Man. That was no taco," Jerry heard the dog say, and he sniggered a bit as they trotted on.

The day had gone on without incident. Lunch was bread and dried fruit. Dinner had been more of the same. Kahuna got sick in the late afternoon, but he seemed fine now. The dog's road-kill snack was probably the cause of his upset tummy. The sun was setting already, and Wizzle had said they still had about an hour to go for the day.

"We're going to stay with an old friend of mine just outside of Amosbury," Wizzle explained. "He *officially* left the Coalition about the same time as Stringer, but he's still a believer in the cause. Name's Thunderhoof. He's a Cherokee Indian. His family's been here for several generations. He's good people."

"I thought the Cherokee's were *American* Indians. What are they doing *here*?" Jerry asked.

"Same as the Bigfoots," Wizzle explained. "Well, not exactly. They aren't running from anyone, but they traveled through the same portals as the old Sasquatch families generations ago. Now this is home for them."

Kahuna had some kind of manic music track playing in his head. Jerry just could not turn off the "NANANANANANANANA" reverberating from the dog's ping-pong ball sized brain.

"What in the world are you humming... or whatever that is that you're doing?" Jerry barked at Kahuna. "I can't get that darned song outta my head."

"Maybe that's because I can't get it out of *my* head." Kahuna answered him. "It's been stuck there for hours."

"Yeah. I know. What is it?" Jerry asked again.

"I think it's called *Wipe Out!*"

That synched it. Jerry now knew that the dog was totally mental. "Isn't that some surfer song from when my grandpa was a little kid?"

"Uh-huh."

"So where did you hear it?"

"Sometimes it plays on the beach music stations where Slash lifeguards," the dog replied.

Jerry nodded. Of course it did. And Jerry noticed that Kahuna usually spoke in the present tense. Slash and his other roommate Jimmy were still just as much a part of Kahuna's present and future as they were of his past. It never even seemed to cross the dog's tiny mind that he might not see them again. Jerry envied him for this. He wished he could be as naive and unencumbered with the weight of worry as his canine companion.

As they got closer to the town, they passed occasional farmhouses with increasing frequency. Most of the windows on these homes glowed warmly from the evening fires inside. Even as cold as the air was outside, the smell of wood fires made Jerry feel warmer and reminded him of home. Then, even though Jerry had been expecting to see teepees, he was still surprised by the size of the Indian village that sprawled out below him. Heck, it was more like a small city.

Wizzle led them through the Native American village around the fires and groups of people who stared at them as they walked by on their ostriches. He led them past congregations of older Indian women sitting on logs, sewing animal skins together who smiled as they walked by. He guided them finally to one of the larger teepees and called, "Hey, Thunderhoof. You in there?" Sometimes, Jerry was still amused at the sound of Wizzle's voice. Even in his biggest voice, the gnome still sounded almost like a kid who had just sucked the gas from a helium balloon.

A tall, dark skinned man with a long, black pony tail folded the door flap back a smidgen, peered out for a moment, then stepped out to greet his old comrade.

"Wizzle! Is good to see you again," Thunderhoof said, reaching out to hug the little man on the big bird.

"It's good to *be* seen. So how's your family?"

"Very good. And Bigger!" He exclaimed proudly. "Runs-with-the-wind has given birth to twin girls since last we spoke."

"Oh! Congratulations," Wizzle said. "So that's 3, then, right?"

"Yes." A boy a little older than Jerry peered out of the teepee. Thunderhoof caught Jerry's eyes glancing at the doorway and turned to see the young man within. "Do you remember young Speaks-to-the-heavens?" The older boy stepped out of the teepee.

Wizzle looked amazed. "Oh. It *has* been a long time, hasn't it?"

"Too long," the Indian agreed. "You bring many friends."

"Yes," Wizzle answered him. "We are taking the boys to meet with Shaymalon."

"Of course. Would you like to rest with my family tonight?"

"Yes. We would like that very much," Wizzle answered. "Let me introduce these fine people to you. I think you might already know Fink?"

Thunderhoof nodded.

"This is Clairese and Jacob McKlesky," Wizzle said.

"It is good to meet you," Thunderhoof said to the fairies.

"This boy is Bobby Schrader, and this is CJ Powell," Wizzle continued.

Thunderhoof nodded again.

"And lastly, this is Jeremiah McAllister," Wizzle said.

"You can call me Jerry, sir," Jerry said without thinking.

"I will, then. It is good of you all to be here with us tonight," Thunderhoof said. One of his neighbors was approaching, probably to see who the strangers were. Thunderhoof walked over to this man and they talked quietly for a moment.

"Oh sure," Jerry heard Kahuna grumble. "No one ever introduces the dog, do they?"

Jerry rolled his eyes and tried to ignore Kahuna's comment.

"My brother will see to your animals," the chief said. The other man was already walking up to Bobby and holding out a hand to help him down.

"Mr. Thunderhoof..." Jerry began.

"Just Thunderhoof."

"Right. Um, sir, would it be okay if Kahuna slept inside with us tonight?"

Fink looked down at the ground and shook his head, but said nothing. The Indian just scratched his head a moment. Finally, he said, "Ah... Yes... That will be alright."

"Good boy, Jerry. If I had a biscuit, I'd give it to *you*," Kahuna said. "No. Strike that. If I had one biscuit, I'd eat it. But if I had two, I'd let you have one of 'em."

"Thunderhoof. Can we talk in private for a moment?" Wizzle whispered to the Indian.

"It has been many moons since we smoked together. Come. We will talk inside."

"Sounds wonderful," Wizzle said

Thunderhoof nodded and helped Wizzle down from his ostrich. They stepped inside the teepee. Jerry knew that Wizzle was instructing his old friend not to talk about their upcoming ordeal, and accepted it. The only thing that helped make it bearable was that he expected that they might get some answers tomorrow night. While Thunderhoof and Wizzle smoked and talked, the boys helped Thunderhoof's brother unload their gear from the ostriches. The Indian took the birds to a stable of sorts where they were fed and watered.

Wizzle emerged from the teepee, followed by Thunderhoof.

"Wizzle says you have much travel ahead. Come. Sleep," Thunderhoof said. He had one arm outstretched as if to say *welcome friends* and a solemn but friendly look on his face. His other arm held the flap open.

It was surprisingly spacious inside. A small fire burned in the middle of the floor. There were two young girls already sleeping on animal furs at the far side of the teepee. A woman sat beside them with a hand on one of the girls. Her smile warmed Jerry to the core. He was instantly transported to a time when he was little and his mother would massage his shoulder while he fell safely off to sleep, his favorite things surrounding him. It was amazing to him how different life was now.

"Come on, Jerry. It's cold out here," Bobby said, and nudged him in the shoulder.

"Oh. Yeah, sorry," Jerry said, startled back to reality. He stepped the rest of the way inside.

Lying on his blanket beside Kahuna that night, Jerry's head was spinning. He was thinking about the coming day. There was going to be another gateway passage. He wasn't sure if he really wanted to do that again, but there wasn't a choice. Besides, in a strange sort of way, he looked forward to it. Then, they were going to fly hundreds of miles on... he couldn't turn his brain off. How he wished he had thought to bring along his CD player. He could get lost in his tunes, and just maybe he could go to sleep. Of course, next he realized that even if he had thought to bring along some music, the player would probably not work in the vicinity of the glowstones. After what seemed like hours lying awake and trying to think of nothing, he finally slipped into the clouds, and he was flying. Not on the back of a Great Golden Hawk, but just holding out his arms, alone. No. Not alone. He was drifting above the clouds and Kahuna was flying beside him. The cool wind was blowing their hair around, and there were occasional mountain peaks poking through. The rest of the night was peaceful sleep, until he opened his eyes again in the morning to find Wizzle standing over him, trying to rouse him from his slumber. As the cobwebs of sleep gave way to the clarity of wakefulness, Jerry felt a thought take shape in his mind. He was going to be on the other side of the world this evening, and he didn't even have a plane ticket.

CHAPTER 14

FLIGHT OF APOLLO

AFTER HE HAD been awake for only a few minutes, the smells of morning brought Jerry completely and fully alive. The mingled scents of coffee, meat cooking and some kind of sweet bread seemed to saturate so deeply into Jerry's body that he could actually taste them. He had not even been aware of being slightly hungry when he went to sleep last night, but now he was famished.

Thunderhoof's wife, Runs-with-the-wind, was leaning over the fire, moving clay pots around. She slid a hot rock out from the coals, and scraped some thick and pasty yellow mush from it onto a plate. She handed this to Jerry. He took it gratefully, and thanked her. Bobby and CJ were awake, and probably had been for a little while. They seemed to have eaten already. There was no sign of the fairies or Kahuna, and Wizzle was talking quietly with Thunderhoof.

They saw Jerry watching them and they each bid him good morning. "How was your sleep, Jerry?" Thunderhoof asked him.

Jerry tried to swallow the food he had just put in his mouth, but it was too hot to chew properly and he chomped at it a couple times, then gulped it down. "Good."

"I see you find Runs-with-the-wind's corncakes acceptable?" Thunderhoof asked.

"They're wonderful," Jerry answered. "But very hot," he added just to make conversation.

"Eat up Jerry," Wizzle said. "We have our longest travel day yet."

"Yeah. I kinda guessed that," Jerry replied.

"Thunderhoof and I were just making the arrangements to get to the gateway. He's going to lend us a few horses, and a couple of his men will ride along. They will bring the horses back when we leave."

"What about the ostriches?" Jerry asked.

"They were released earlier this morning," Thunderhoof assured him.

Jerry was glad to hear that the birds were free. He went back to work on his breakfast, and got ready to depart.

Leaving the village on horseback, Jerry and his friends were treated like royalty. They had been offered armloads of jewelry and other trinkets as well as several hand-woven blankets to take with them. Wizzle thanked them for the generous offers, but explained that they would have to travel lightly. Some of the Indians were waving and tagging along like the people who follow the last float in a parade, just trying to savor the last minutes of the festivities. A couple of the Indian girls had even come close just to touch the hands of the travelers, wave and run giggling away.

The teepee village gave way to more traditional homes. Before long, taller buildings lined both sides of cobblestone streets. Some had heavy, rough-hewn timbers that framed white stucco in geometric patterns. Their gingerbready roof peaks finished off the whole Scandinavian theme. Jerry felt highly self-conscious, walking through town with Indians, gnomes and fairies, but no one seemed to take any notice of them at all.

Several blocks later, the architecture started to change again. Old Denmark gave way to Old Arabia. Tan stucco buildings, with open archways and canvas awnings flanked the street. One street to the right spread out wider than the rest and a confusing mass of canopy roofs and tents filled it, selling everything from fruits and breads, to clothes. At a nearby stand, a merchant sold small models of Stonehenge and little stone earrings shaped like the monolithic Easter Island statues that watched eternally out to sea. The people milling about in the bazaar were all dressed differently. Some were Middle-eastern in white robes with turbans on their heads. There were gnomes in business suits, and bald women in what looked like metallic jumpsuits. Dozens of different cultures lived together here, and not all of them were human. Though the assortment amazed Jerry, to these people, this diversity was ordinary.

As they turned to the right, their destination loomed about a block in front of them. The street opened up onto what appeared to be a broad grassy park. Two massive oaks framed the end of the block. The park beyond was dressed with more trees, benches, tables, pavilions and swing sets. The cobbled paving stones gave way to a wide, pea gravel path that led straight to the center of the park, where there stood a stunning ancient ruin. Stonehenge, in all its mystic glory, rose from a circular mound like a sacred temple. But far from being in ruin, this looked like it could have been constructed yesterday. Many of the people in Stonehenge Park were walking towards or away from the circle of stone pillars, most carrying some kinds of baggage, some with small children in tow. The most striking thing, however, was the swirling mass of colorful mist in the center of it all. It was very much like the mist that the boys had passed through as they entered the realm of Tellusia, but this was not contained in a small doorway. This covered almost the entire area within the great stone circle. As people entered between the columns, they walked into the mist and disappeared. Other people just walked from the vaporous energy ball as if they were entering this world from another dimension, which of course they might have been. There were uniformed sentries posted at each column, and at the end of each of the six pathways entering the portal, there were small booths with a few people lined up at each.

"This doorway's a little trickier than the one you boys came through, but nothing to be concerned about," Wizzle said to the boys. "Before we walk into the gateway, we will have to stop at the routing booth. There we will each receive a necklace with a pass stone that's keyed to our destination. Without one of these, there is no telling where we would end up today."

"What about us?" Jacob asked.

Wizzle thought for a moment then said, "I guess we will just have to asked the routing agent."

He turned to Thunderhoof. "Old friend. Your kindness has once again left me just wishing for more time to spend with you and your family. Thank you for all you have done for us."

"It was a pleasure and an honor," Thunderhoof answered. "May the Great Spirit protect and guide you on your journey."

"Thank you," Wizzle said to the Indian. They all climbed down from their horses, shook hands, hugged and said their final goodbyes. Then, the boys walked towards the gateway with the gnomes and the fairies and the dog, while the Indians stood watching with their horses.

At the routing booth, they waited a few minutes for the attendant to finish with a family in front of them. When it was their turn, Wizzle stepped up onto a raised platform and spoke to her. "Good morning, ma'am." She muttered a bored Hello and

Wizzle continued. "We have a total of eight traveling to Inzia today. We are two gnomes, three human boys, two fairies and a dog."

Jerry expected her to get flustered with Mr. surfer-dog and the fairies, but she never missed a beat. With all the panache of a tollbooth attendant on the turnpike, she handed out six necklac-es Jerry considered to be a regular size, and two more that would have been tight around his index finger. "Put these around your necks, then follow this path to the fourth column on the right. When the mist turns blue, you may all enter together. Next." A tall man with a brief case waited for them to move aside then stepped up to be waited on by Ms. Sunshine.

"And you said *I* had an attitude," Kahuna conveyed to Jerry.

As they approached the portal entrance, Jerry started to get that familiar all-is-right-with-the-world feeling again. What looked like a family of furry balls with arms and legs emerged from the next doorway to the right, making odd squeaking and hooting sounds as they seemed to be verifying that they had all came out together.

Wizzle gave the go ahead, and they all stepped towards the mist.

"Well, see ya on the other side, buddy," Bobby said to Jerry.

Jerry hung a necklace around Kahuna's neck. He heard the dog ask, "Like, what's goin' on here?"

"Just stay with me, boy. It's okay," Jerry said. They stepped into the mist, and time faded away. In what could have been two seconds or two decades later, Jerry came out the other side. Fink and Bobby were already waiting. CJ, Kahuna and the fairies came out behind him. Finally Wizzle materialized, and they huddled together, taking in the sights and sounds.

It was quite a bit warmer, and cloudy. Jerry hadn't even no-ticed how sunny it had been in Amosbury until he stepped out of the portal. They had been ejected onto the sidewalk of a town in Inzia called Bhokatta. Much like the city they had left, there were many cultures represented in the dress and architecture of Bhokatta, but the buildings were jumbled up. They had been divided into neighborhoods in Amosbury, but not here. Directly across the street was an Old Western saloon built adjacent to a small French bakery. A modern American style convenience store shared the saloon's wall on the other side. Wizzle collected the pass stones and returned them to the routing agent. He and the attendant mumbled a few things to each other, then Wizzle rejoined his friends.

"He said that we could find our hawk at the livery stables down the street," Wizzle said, looking around at the rest of the crew. They all turned to look behind themselves. Sure enough, about a block away, the head of a colossal bird could be seen above the buildings. They started off to meet their connecting flight.

* * * * *

"Great Golden Hawk? Yeah, you can have her" The stable owner said. He was a smallish man, probably Jerry's father's age. His cowboy hat covered his skull, but was not as large as the old Texas 10-gallon variety, and his eyes exuded the confidence of a man who knew his own heart. "It's all I can do to keep her from eating the other animals. Do you know how much one of these things eats? Thank goodness she had that muzzle on her beak," He said.

"I can only imagine," Wizzle replied, handing him some kind of currency.

"She had a note with her. It says that her name is Apollo," The man said.

Jerry heard CJ mumble something and asked him what he said.

"I think Apollo was the name of the Greek God that carried the sun across the sky everyday."

"Indeed," said Wizzle.

The old cowboy led them through the stables and into a corral. The massive animal filled the pen so completely that it was hard to imagine her having enough room to spread her wings. A box like a small trolley car was harnessed onto her back, and she looked ready get the heck outta Dodge City.

"Would ya look at the size of that chicken?" Kahuna exclaimed. "I'm, like getting hungry just thinking 'bout it."

"Is everything always about food with you?" Jerry noted.

"Dude, what else *is* there?"

Jerry shook his head.

The stable keeper walked back into the livery building, and returned with a ladder. The hawk was lying perfectly still on her stomach, but with every breath, the transport car rose and fell several inches. "I'll hold the ladder," he said, "And y'all can climb up onto her back. From there, you should have no trouble entering the car from the rear."

Jerry looked down at Kahuna. "How 'bout you?" He asked.

"I'll carry him up," The cowboy said.

"Oh, goodie," Jerry heard Kahuna mutter.

When they were all seated and strapped in, the stable manager unbuckled the muzzle that Apollo had on her beak. Then, she stood up and he unlocked the chain from her ankle. Everything was still for a moment, and then with all the force of a volcano, or an avalanche, she exploded in slow motion into the air. They dropped several feet and, before they had a chance to register what was going on, they were being thrust back up. Then stopped. Then up. Then stopped. Then up, and up, and up. CJ and Bobby were screaming, and Jerry laughed and hollered in the same breath each time the wings thrust them farther into the air. He was holding his lurching stomach, which tickled even more now than it did on the first big drop of his favorite roller coaster.

From his window, Jerry watched the ground fall away fast. In less than a minute Bhokatta looked more like a bunch of models than a real town. Bhokatta had been built on a hillside that overlooked a wide majestic river. There were farmer's fields in every direction, and straight irrigation canals divided the land into a multi-shaded green checkerboard. In no time at all, they were lifting into the low cloud cover, and the surface of Tellusia vanished below them as all the compartment windows turned solid gray.

With nothing to look at, everyone turned his or her attention back to the inner cabin. Inside the mile high trolley car, Bobby said, "Whoa. I don't know what I was expecting, but that wasn't it."

"Oh Man, that was *so* cool," CJ exclaimed.

"I think I'm gonna yak," Kahuna said. Jerry turned to look at the dog sharing his seat, and the poor animal was shaking and cowering. Each time the bird drove her wings against the air, the car leaned back and was thrust forward in a motion that could have made Popeye seasick. And if that weren't enough, Jerry's ears felt like someone was sticking pencils in them.

"It's okay, Kahuna. You'll be okay." He put his hand on the dog's neck and kneaded it with his fingertips.

"Man, why does everybody always say that?" The dog asked. He was miserable.

Jerry shook his head. *Why* does *everybody always say that* he wondered? "I don't know buddy. I don't know."

Jacob and Clairese seemed to be using the flight time to sleep. They had taken refuge in the pockets of CJ's jacket, which lay on the seat beside him. Wizzle, who was sitting in front of Jerry, turned around to face him. "So, what do you think of flying?"

"Well, I've flown before, but it has never been like this. I'm going to need a barf bag."

"Oh my gosh!" Wizzle exclaimed suddenly. "I forgot all about these." Wizzle reached deep into his jacket somewhere and brought out a handful of small pellets.

"What are those?" Jerry inquired.

"Compressed Da-Da weed," Wizzle said.

"What are they for?"

"Motion sickness," Wizzle answered. He handed one to Jerry. "Put it in your mouth."

Jerry surveyed it for a moment. It looked like it came from a box of moldy Choco-Puffs cereal. He put it on his tongue, and knew right away that it was not chocolate flavored cereal. It tasted like grass. The pellet opened on his tongue, and he could feel the leaf fragments unraveling and then lying there. The nausea was subsiding already, and he hadn't even swallowed anything yet. Wizzle handed Jerry another, and motioned for him to give it to Kahuna.

Within moments, everyone had eaten a Da-Da pellet and there was no more talk of motion sickness. It had even alleviated the discomfort in Jerry's ears caused by the rapid changes in air pressure.

"Dude," Kahuna imparted to Jerry. "Tell Wizzle I said thanks."

Breaking though the cloud canopy, they squinted against the brilliance of full sunlight. From below, the clouds had been gray and depressing. Here on top, they were white, soft and peaceful.

Apollo's wings beat out a slow rhythm with immeasurable force, loud whooshing sounds accompanying each stroke like a blacksmith's bellows. When she would stop and hold her wings out to let herself float on a thermal column, the near silence rang in their ears louder than the whooshing had been before. The only sound was a quiet whistle of the air pressing against the glass, or leaking in through a small hole near the door. Apollo hung on the air, seemingly still, for several minutes. As a mountain peak sailed past with surprising speed, it became evident that they were not motionless. It had been a small island in the vast ocean of clouds, and in no time at all, it shrank to a minute bump poking through the clouds behind them.

As the day wore on, the scenery changed repeatedly. Jerry woke from a well-deserved nap to find that they had left the cloud cover behind. They soared above huge tracts of arid and dusty plains. Moving north, the ground cover started showing patches of white where earlier clouds had dispatched great armies of snowflakes to lay siege to the land.

In front of them lay a magnificent mountain range that stretched out to the horizon on the right and left.

"The Hummalinos," Wizzle said to the boys. "We'll follow these mountains here northwest for another hour or so, then we'll touchdown in Zaharania."

"That's in Neepol, right?" CJ asked.

"Yep," Wizzle confirmed. "It's a little town, so it's pretty quiet. That's how he likes it."

"He?" Jerry wondered aloud.

"You know, Shaymalon. The guy lives for silence. And the snow around the village soaks up most of the stray sound when the wind is calm."

Their flying trolley car did have glass windows, but no heat, so the cold air outside had pried its way into the cabin. Frost framed the edges of each windowpane. They were using blankets they had found stored in a trunk by the door. Fully dressed for winter and covered with one of these heavy wool blankets, Jerry still shivered from the air moving through the drafty coach.

Bobby turned away from his window and asked Fink, "So, what is Zaharania like?"

"Cold, for one thing. In summer, the temperature rarely gets above zero. And in winter, whoa! Sometimes it drops to minus 50," Fink explained.

"Fahrenheit?" CJ asked.

"What?" Fink asked back.

"Is that Fahrenheit or Centigrade?" CJ rephrased the question.

"I think it's Centigrade," Fink replied.

"That's good," CJ said.

"Why's that?" Jerry asked.

"Well, I guess it doesn't really matter," CJ answered.

"Oh no. Here he goes again," Bobby whined.

"What?" CJ asked.

"Oh nothing," Bobby said. Then he leaned over and jokingly whispered to Jerry loud enough for everyone to hear, "I think we're about to get one of CJ's science lessons."

"Hey!" CJ said. He feigned indignation, but it was obvious that CJ was truly proud of the knowledge he possessed. He explained the relationship between the Fahrenheit and the Centigrade scales for several minutes. Jerry was sure that some people would find it fascinating, but he just found it droll.

When CJ finally stopped talking, Bobby said. "So what he's trying to say is that it is going to be cold. Come to think of, I think Fink said that, like an hour ago."

"So, why would anyone want to live in a place like this?" Bobby asked.

"To be left alone, of course," Fink answered.

"What do you mean?" Bobby asked. "Are there people trying to destroy you or something?"

Fink deflected the question. "Well, yes and no. But that's a story for later."

Wizzle, who had been quiet all this time said, "There are other reasons to seek isolation."

"Like what?" Jerry asked.

"Peace," Wizzle answered.

"But you just said we weren't going to talk about your enemies just yet," Bobby said.

"I don't mean peace among peoples. I mean peace of the spirit. Solitude."

Bobby looked confused, but Jerry thought he understood.

Wizzle continued, "To put it simply, peace comes from acceptance: acceptance of others outside yourself; acceptance of the circumstances that move your life and the lives of those around you. But mostly, it is a product of accepting yourself; of loving yourself."

Bobby looked lost. Wizzle continued, "It's one of those things that you can't understand until you've had a taste of it, Bobby. It's like the man who was blind from birth. He has never seen before, so he can't imagine what sight is like. Those who seek peace are like men who were born with sight, but lost it in later years. They know what vision was like, and would give anything to experience it again."

"Do you live there?" Jerry asked Wizzle. "I mean in Zaharania?"

"Heavens, no," Wizzle said. "I can't stand that kind of cold."

"Then where are you from?" Jerry asked him. It had never crossed his mind to consider where they were from. He had assumed that they just lived in Sconelund. Of course, now that he thought about it, Wizzle didn't have a Scottish accent. Then he wondered if that meant anything in this alternate reality.

Wizzle explained where he lived in Tellusian terms. It sounded like it was in the Western United States, maybe in central California. Jerry pictured a bustling village in the foothills of the Rocky Mountains where the flowers bloomed in late February, instead of waiting for March and April like the rest of the Northern Hemisphere. Fink explained that he had also come from the village where Wizzle lived and Fink talked of their friendship.

"And then there was that time the mountain lion went after Wizzle," Fink went on. "I thought he was going to cry. He was running as fast as his squatty little legs would go. If you've ever seen one of us run, you'll know. It's not pretty. The mountain lion should have had him, I pulled out a schlinger and a zarch, and let the big cat have it right on her haunches. You should have seen her!" He was laughing as he spoke. "She threw her paws out in front of her to stop, but she must have got one of them caught on a tree root or something. She flipped over and into the air, landing right on my old buddy. Well, Wiz' here, dragged himself out from under the struggling animal while she tried to get at that zarch dangling off her back side, and he started running again. By the time she's up again, Wizzle throws himself into an abandoned burrow of some kind, and the lion, ha, aha, she never even slows down. Heh, heh. She shoves her head into the hole and all you can hear is a muffled cat crying to get free." Fink wiped his fingers under his eyes where tears had rolled down his cheeks from laughing so hard. "A couple minutes later, Wizzle crawls out a hole a few meters away, and in his indignation, he picks up a little stick and swats her on the behind, yelling *Bad kitty! Bad, bad kitty!*"

"Well, it served her right!" Wizzle said. "She would have taken me home to feed the cubs. Jeesh. Predators."

"Dude. I love a cat story with an unhappy ending," Kahuna said in Jerry's head.

Jerry giggled.

"Hey, what's that smoke over there?" CJ said. He had been looking out the front window. Apollo's wings beat in the slow, constant rhythm that she had been doing for most of the past seven hours or so. The horizon bobbed in and out of sight each time she thrust her wings against the air again. For an instant, Jerry, and the rest of them, could see the smoke, and then it was gone again, then visible, then gone, and so on.

"I think that's Zaharania," Wizzle said.

"Why all the smoke?" CJ asked.

"It's cold. A fire in the fireplace will help keep that cold at bay," Wizzle answered.

"Must be a lot of fireplaces," CJ said. They moved closer by the minute.

"I don't know, Wizzle," Fink said warily. "That is a lot of smoke."

Wizzle looked quietly out the front window for a bit, taking in the view each time the horizon reappeared over the mammoth hawk's head. Finally he said, "I don't like it."

Several silent moments passed, then in unison, CJ, Bobby and Fink gasped. Jerry saw it too. The smoke was rising into the air thick and black. And there were flames visible at the base of the column of smoke, 20 feet high, maybe more. It was hard to know at this distance. They all watched helplessly, as the Great Golden Hawk took them closer to the town in the mountains.

"It's probably a house fire," Wizzle said to reassure them.

"Yeah. That happens, you know," Fink continued, climbing onto the on the same train of thought that Wizzle had just sent out of the station. “A spark from someone’s fireplace probably just jumped onto the curtains.”

Wizzle said, “Could be a thousand things. Maybe a candle was carelessly left on a kitchen table to burn down onto a stack of papers.”

Seeing where they were going with this, CJ added, “Or maybe someone was smoking in bed. You know. They fell asleep and their cigarette started the mattress burning. Happens all the time.”

“No one smokes cigarettes here, but maybe a pipe,” Fink said.

“It’s not just one home,” Jerry said solemnly. He was right. Several buildings were engulfed in flames.

“Well, in town, the houses do share common walls. It could just spread from one to the next like dominos,” Wizzle conceded.

“But, it’s on both sides of the street,” Jerry said.

“Forest fires can jump a 100 foot fire break to continue on the other side,” CJ reported. “Maybe some sparks drifted across the street and started the next house going.”

Everyone wanted to believe the fires were caused by a careless mistake, but they knew. They all knew. The timing and location was too perfect to be a coincidence.

They approached from the south, and the smoke was drifting north, so they weren’t flying through it. But the air was still heavy with the acrid smell of it. It was like a wood fire in a fireplace, only a hundred times stronger, maybe a thousand times stronger. Apollo held her wings out to her sides and glided in closer to the ground, then leaned way back and with several quick flaps, she brought them to a gentle landing. Apollo instantly assumed her natural standing position in the square at the end of town. She was still situated in such a way that her head blocked much of the municipality from their view.

"Stay here," Wizzle said firmly to everyone in the cabin. "Clairese, come with me. Fink, if I send her back, you get them out of here immediately." With that, he was out the back door and gone from view.

When Wizzle reappeared in the street below them, a gnome dressed in a red and white suit greeted him. With his long white beard and red hat, he could have passed for Santa Clause, but he somehow didn't look quite jolly enough. Maybe that had something to do with the fact that his entire town was ablaze.

"That's Mayor Schnitski," Fink reported. The man handed Wizzle a note with a jagged hole in it, and as he read it, the mayor talked and frantically gestured towards the town behind him. Wizzle looked up a time or two from the page he was reading, then went back to the note with Clairese looking over his shoulder. When he was done, Wizzle and Schnitski talked more. As they started to walk out of view, Clairese flew back into the cabin.

"The fires were no accident," she said. "They were attacked by a band of Yetis about two hours ago."

"We gotta get outta here," Fink said, but before he could signal the bird to lift off, Clairese stopped him by holding her hands out like a crossing guard.

"Schnitski says it's okay. They're long gone," she said.

Fink was momentarily quiet, then asked, "Was anyone hurt?"

"About 10 or 12 people, but mostly minor injuries. They'll be alright. The town doctor is already seeing to their needs," she answered. "But, they took Shaymalon with them."

"What?" Fink asked, needing confirmation.

"Fink. They took Shaymalon. And they tacked a note up on the temple door with a knife holding it in place," Clairese said. Tiny little tears rolled from her eyes.

Jerry's heart sank. He didn't need to hear what she was going to say because somehow, he already knew. He wasn't sure she would even be able to say the words, so he spoke for her. "The note says, *Deliver Jerry, or Shaymalon dies.*"

Except for the howl of the wind and the crackle of the flames beyond, the compartment was silent. The odd thing was that no one seemed surprised. Before anyone even had a chance to react, a number of soldiers surrounded the bird. The leader was a gnome woman with shiny black hair who scrambled up the ladder and yanked the door open.

"Get out now and follow me!" she barked. Her green eyes flashed – *was that hatred* – at Jerry.

Bobby opened his mouth to speak, but she cut him short. "No questions now. Just go!"

There was to be no discussing it with this woman. She marched into the car and around behind them. She seemed to be searching the compartment as if confirming that there was no one hiding under a seat or a blanket. Again, she shouted at them, almost shrieking. "Go on! Move!"

Jerry was beginning to wonder if his days might be numbered. If this woman was, in any way, representative of the local population, they must have held him responsible for the attack on Zaharania. And why wouldn't they? The attack was surely sparked by his foretold arrival. That would make the destruction and the injuries his fault. The ransom note plainly stated that Shaymalon was taken because of him. Jerry, of course, had never done anything to them, but in the heat of anger, people rarely see things reasonably. He was becoming more and more certain that the locals would turn him over to Inar if they thought it might get their beloved Shaymalon back. He didn't even realize he was just standing in place until the leader of the Gnomish guard poked him in the back and screamed, "Would you please get moving?"

That did it. He made for the exit. He was even more certain now that they were going to hand him over, but stalling might only make things worse on him and his friends. The trade could happen in two hours, or it might be two days, but he knew it was coming.

He pushed out of the door and gazed into the red glow of the setting sun.

*****

This is the end of Book One.
We hope you have enjoyed the story so far. For a preview of *Jerry McAllister and the Slaves of the Tellusian Underground: Book Two*, please visit:

www.tadparker.com/10701.html

Once there, you will be invited to preview the next chapter. You may also purchase your own copy at a significant discount. So, what are you waiting for? Take a look. Read on. And if your parents agree, pick up Book Two today.

Breinigsville, PA USA
01 April 2010
235329BV00002B/2/P

9 781935 267027